Sara McNeil:
A New Beginning

By Master Coe

EAN/ISBN-13: 978-1-60965-015-5 (paperback)

EAN/ISBN-13: 978-1-60965-016-2 (digital eBook)

EAN/ISBN-13: 978-1-60965-017-9 (enhanced digital eBook)

Publisher: MC Publications

1042 N. Mountain Ave, Suite B-231

Upland, CA 91786

http://www.MCPublications-Books.com

Cover designed by Master Coe.

Cover photo licensed by Nevest. Model release is on file.

Vol. 3

Sara McNeil Series

Table of Contents

Rise and Shine

Of course by now you know that I'm Sara McNeil. This term has been a roller coaster for me. I thought I really blew it with my Mistress, but things seemed to have worked themselves out. I just have one final to complete and then it will be time for a long awaited summer break.

Mistress Yvonne has plans for us this summer. I don't know what they are. I'm hoping she will tell me tonight when she gets home. I originally planned on veg'ing out at home this summer. It will be good to get out and do stuff.

I don't have to be in class until one o'clock this afternoon so the plan was to sleep in. But Mistress made waffles and now I can't go back to bed until I finish cleaning up. Technically I could, but who wants to wake up to a mess. I'm glad she isn't one of those messy cooks.

Just as I got the dishwasher loaded and running someone is knocking at my door. Shit and I'm not even dressed. Mistress insisted on me wearing nothing this morning and I hadn't had a chance to get dressed.

"Just a moment," I yell out as I scramble to find some clothing.

"Open up bitch, its dark out here. Your hallway is fucking creepy."

What the fuck is Justine doing here?

I grab a towel and wrap it around me and open the door. Justine walks in as if she owns the place, "Well come-the-fuck in why don't you?"

"What happened to the lights?"

"They went out a week ago. I thought you had finals this morning?"

"I had my last final yesterday. It smells good in here." Justine tosses her jacket on the sofa and sits down. "I didn't mean to interrupt your shower. Go ahead and shower, I'll wait."

9

"Mistress made waffles. I wasn't about to shower."

"So you always walk around wearing only a towel?"

"I was about to go back to bed for a few hours. Why are you here?"

"I was going to ask you to breakfast."

"I can make you some eggs if you want. I'm sorry but the waffles are gone."

Justine stood up and walked over to me. She removed my towel and let it fall to the ground. I wish I could say I resisted, but there is something about her that makes me go weak. She takes me by my waist and pulls me into her. "I'm not really all that hungry."

I can feel her breath against my lips. "I can't. I have to rest. I have finals."

She kisses me gently on the lips. She pulls away so her lips are lightly touching mine. She whispers, "So let's go rest together."

I swear she is the horniest cunt I ever met. "I have to be up by eleven thirty."

"So set an alarm. Besides if you went to sleep now you will be too sleepy for your exam." She let the straps from her dress fall off her shoulders. She pulled her dress down past her hips and stepped out of it. Her bra was the next to fall to the ground and she was stepping out of her panties as she led me to my bedroom.

"I really have to rest." I may have been more convincing if I wasn't eagerly hopping into bed at the time.

Justine sat on the side of the bed and pulled off her shoes and socks. She set the alarm clock and climbed into bed and cuddled next to me and wrapped her incredibly long legs around me. "I just want to cuddle."

I was actually hopping she wanted to do more than just to cuddle, but I didn't care. I love the way her body feels against mine. Truth-be-told I get wet just thinking about her and that perfect dancer's body.

Usually Justine is a very aggressive lover. For some reason she just laid there with her body tightly wrapped around me. "Is everything alright?" I asked.

She didn't answer right away. "I'm fine." She buried her head deep into my shoulders.

I knew she was lying and I would have pressed the issue, but the phone rang. Justine loosened her grip on me as I reached back and answered the phone. "Hello."

"Oh good you're still up, mi amante." My Mistress Yvonne answered from the other end of the phone.

"Yes Mistress, I am still awake."

Of course Justine chose that moment to start kissing down my neck towards my chest.

"I ran into an old friend of mine and we are going out tonight. I want you to dress to impress." Mistress sounded very excited.

Just as I was answering, Justine sucked my entire left breast into her mouth. My voice quivered and cracked as I answered Mistress. "Ye – yes Mistress."

"Are you alright?"

"Uh-huh." I normally would have said more, but Justine ran the tip of her tongue around my very sensitive nipple.

"You sound distracted. Is Justine there with you?"

I struggled to regain my composure. "Yes Mistress, Justine is here with me."

Justine lifted her head up just long enough to greet my Mistress. "Good morning Mistress Yvonne." She waved her hand as to say hello, as if Mistress could see her. What a goofball. Justine wasted no time she started kissing down the middle of my stomach.

Mistress voice went from giddy to concerned, for the lack of a better word. "You really should be getting ready for your exam and

11

not fucking around. If you blow this exam, your ass is mine. Am I making myself clear?"

"Yes Mistress."

"I swear I don't know what goes through that head of yours sometimes. Usted me preocupa a veces."

I'm not quite sure what she said in that last sentence, but it didn't sound good. To make things worse Justine had just forced my legs apart and was using her tongue to invade my pussy. "I'll be good Mistress." Oh yeah … like that last blurb made sense.

"I have to go. I'll see you later this evening."

Mistress hung up before I could respond. I set the phone down and sat up. "Shit. She sounded pissed."

I could see the lack of any real concern in Justine's face. "What did she say?"

"She said not to blow my final."

Justine pulled me back down onto my back by my legs. "So don't blow your test."

I pulled my knees together. "I think we should stop."

Justine sighed, "Did she say to stop?"

"Not exactly, but she knows you're here."

"They know we fuck around. It's not like we keep it secret from them."

"I know, but I feel guilty."

"What do you feel guilty about?"

"About us, we're cheating on them."

"First off we are not cheating on them. They know we get together and they have even joined in at times."

"I really should study."

"Whatever." Justine got up and started getting dressed.

I sat up and pulled my knees to my chest. "I'm sorry I just don't want to fuck up again."

"I know. No worries, it's cool."

"Are you angry with me?"

She leaned over and kissed me on my forehead. "I'm not angry, I'm horny I need to get fucked."

"I just don't want to let Mistress down again."

"I Know." She started to walk out of the room.

"You don't have to go." Can I get any more pathetic?

"I'm going down to the café. Do you want something?"

"I can make coffee for us here."

"I need to get out get some fresh air and let you get dressed before I rape you." She flashed that wicked smile of hers.

"The problem is that it wouldn't be much of a rape. I really do want to be with you, but Mistress is right. I really should study."

"I'm getting a caramel latte. I'll bring you back a large mocha and one of those dry ass maple scones you like."

"My wallet is in my purse by the door. The least I can do is pay."

"No worries. Just be dressed when I return. I don't know if I can control myself with you walking around naked."

I sat in bed as I heard the door close behind Justine. I got up got dressed and made the bed. When Justine returned we just sat around and made small talk until the alarm in my room went off. I can't study just before a test, it overloads my brain and I always seem to study the wrong things.

"I forgot about the alarm." I got up and started walking into the bedroom. "You can walk me to class if you have time?"

Justine waited until I returned before answering. "How long is your final?"

13

"Three hours, but it shouldn't take me that long."

"Why don't I drive us back to my place? I have some books I need to turn back into the library. I can drive us to campus. I'll meet you in the student center and maybe we can catch a movie or something afterwards?"

"Yeah, I'd like that. I need to unwind a bit before tonight."

"What's happening tonight?"

"Mistress met up with an old friend and I guess we're going out."

"Did she say who it was?"

"Nope," I walked towards the door and picked up my purse. "We better get going."

Justine picked up her keys from the coffee table and followed behind me. She stuck her head out of the door and looked up and down the hallway before stepping out into the dark hallway.

I really don't know why she drove since she lives only a block away. But if I had a cherry red convertible Mustang I would drive everywhere also.

As we pulled up to the driveway of the house Justine and Mistress Kimberly were renting, Mistress Kimberly was walking out the front door. She walked over to the car as we were stepping out. "Whatever trouble the two of you are planning, you need to be home by five, Justine."

"Yes Mistress, may I ask why?" Justine replied.

"We're going out with Yvonne and Sara." Mistress Kimberly pulled a loose string from my blouse. "That goes for you too Sara. The two of you will dress here. We will meet Yvonne at the restaurant."

"Yes ma'am. I'll bring an outfit with me."

"No, come as you are. I'm going to pick out your outfits now."

"Oh how kinky!" Justine blurted out.

14

Mistress Kimberly kissed Justine on her lips. "Just stay out of trouble and don't be late."

"Yes Mistress." Justine responded in a sultry tone.

I so wish I had her confidence. I've been doing this for over a year now. I shouldn't be so intimidated by everything and everyone. Mistress Kimberly drove off in Justine's car since we blocked her in.

I waited until she drove off before I said anything. "How are we going to get to my final in time? She took your car."

Justine holds up the key to Mistress Kimberly's car, which was on her key chain. "We'll take her car." She walked towards her door. "Come on."

I followed as she unlocked the door. I stepped into the house but waited by the doorway while Justine collected her books. "Do you guys always drive whichever car you want?"

"Our driveway is narrow. So instead of always having to wait for the other to move their car we just drive which ever car isn't blocked in."

"That makes sense, but what about insurance?"

Justine came from the back room carrying her books. "We found a cool broker. He set it up so we are both covered under one policy for both cars. He listed us as domestic partners." She opened the door, "Are you ready?"

I nodded and walked out the door.

Final Exams

I forget what we talked about on the drive to campus. The final was a breeze. I was done in an hour and a half. I walked over to the student center to meet Justine. As usual I found her surrounded by a group of black guys. For a lesbian she sure does attract a lot of men and she seems to have a thing for black men.

I caught Justine's eye and waved for her to come with me. She motioned for me to go over to where she was but I refused. So, she excused herself and walked over to me, taking her time taunting her victims with each step she took.

"Why do you do that?" I asked.

"Do what?" She was playing dumb. She knew damn well what I was talking about.

"Why do you tease them like that? Don't you think it's dangerous?"

"Those guys are harmless."

"They don't look harmless to me."

Justine looked at her watch. "It's almost three. Let's go to the café by the quad and then head over to my place."

Before I could answer I was being lead off arm-in-arm by Justine. I looked back to see what the guys were doing. They had split up and some moved on to other girls. "Doesn't it bother you that they can talk to you one moment and then start hitting on another girl as soon as you walk away?"

"You get too attached. It's not like I'm going to do anything with them. That's what I have you for. You are my personal booty call."

She actually patted my bottom. I've never been referenced as a booty call before. "I don't understand why our Mistresses don't have a problem with us getting together?"

"I told you we are sister slaves. Besides they are most likely fucking each other's brains out every chance they get."

I don't know why but the thought of them together made me jealous. Not like I thought Mistress would leave me for her, but that she was with her without me. "I want to be her source of pleasure."

"What?"

Oh shit did I say that out loud? "Nothing, I didn't say anything."

"Yes you did, you jealous little cunt." Justine started laughing at me. "I can show you how to be that for her. But once you do, you can never go back."

"What do you mean?"

Justine opened the door to the café. "We'll talk more when we get home. It's too much to get into right now."

I didn't want to let it go, but I knew she was right. I really didn't want everyone in the café up in my personal business. "I'm buying."

"Cool."

As usual Justine got a latte, nonfat of course, and I got a mocha and maple scone. I swear maple scones are the greatest food ever created. I think I love the smell more than the taste.

We looked around but couldn't find a place to sit so Justine suggested, "We really should be getting back."

"Yeah, it is getting late."

Of course Justine had to park at the very end of the parking lot. We could have walked home in the time it took us to get to her car. On top of that we spent five minutes looking for her car, because Justine forgot she drove Mistress Kimberly's car.

We pulled into the driveway just behind Mistress Kimberly. I wouldn't say she was in a bad mood, but she was definitely stressed. She got out of the car holding two dress bags. "Good you are back. Both of you go shower and I'll be in with your outfits."

I know it really wasn't my place to ask, but not knowing was killing me. "Excuse me Mistress Kimberly, but who are we meeting tonight?"

"That's not your business. Just go get ready." Mistress Kimberly is known to be a bitch. But this time she came across as more nervous than bitchy. Whomever we were going to meet had to be someone very important to Mistress Yvonne and Mistress Kimberly.

I knew better than to say anything more. I stayed close to Justine and followed her to the master bedroom. I sat down as Justine started undressing.

Justine glanced over at me, "Do you plan on showering in your clothes?"

"No. I'll just wait until you're done."

"Bitch, get your silly ass undressed. We don't have time to shower separately. When Mistress is like this it doesn't take much to piss her off."

I stood up and started undressing. Although I no longer had the fear of Mistress Kimberly I had when I first met her, I still get nervous around her and I may have already pissed her off.

Now I enjoy a steamy shower, but I never had a shower spill steam out of the door before I get in. I have never been on a shower quite like this one before. It had four shower heads, one in the front, one in the back and two on the side. The shower heads on the side detached so you can move it all around your body. Each of the heads could be set to pulsate.

Justine turned so I can wash her back. I poured some body soap onto one of those organic sponges and soaped down her back. I was going to stop at her lower back, but she slightly stuck her ass out and I couldn't resist. I knelt down and soaped her tight ass. She spread her legs apart as I slowly worked my way down between her thighs. I so wanted her, but I dared not risk it.

Justine let out a frustrated sigh, turned around and pulled me up by my hair. She pushed me backwards and pinned me against the back of the shower wall. The water from the nozzle above us ran down over my head and face.

Justine pressed her body against mine forcing her right leg between my legs, forcing me to spread my legs and expose my throbbing pussy to the mercy of her probing fingers. I opened my mouth to protest (well maybe not to protest) and she leaned in and kissed me full on the mouth. Her tongue invaded my open mouth.

She removed her fingers from deep inside me and shoved them into my mouth, forcing me to suck my juices from her fingers. That wasn't so bad, it was just unexpected. What was even more unexpected was when she spun me around and pushed me face first into the shower wall.

She soaped my back with the organic sponge. She worked her way down pass my ass and spread my legs apart. She gripped my ass cheeks and spread them so far apart I could feel the warm water run across my opened ass hole. Her narrow tongue quickly invaded my parted anus.

I knew I should have resisted, but I bit down on my lower lip, arched my back and offered my ass up to her freely and willingly. It felt strange to have her tongue invade my ass hole so deep. I could feel myself on the verge of a full orgasm. I was so close to orgasm I could feel my legs weakening beneath me.

I lost it when she pulled my hips out and invaded my cunt with her tongue. I don't know how but she held me securely in place as my entire body quivered and quaked as my insides erupted in pleasure and passion.

She stood up, turned me around and pinned me against the shower wall. She slowly and seductively licked my juices from around her lips, while holding me securely by the back of my hair.

Justine lifted her long right leg up against the shower wall. Her foot was almost even with my shoulder. She forced me down to my

19

knees and forced my face between her legs. The fully extended leg left her pussy open. I could smell her sex as she forced my mouth over her slimy cunt.

I had forgotten how wet Justine can get. I lapped up every drop of her creamy cum. I don't know how she held her balance. I could feel her body quiver as my tongue circled her exposed clitoris.

We were so into the moment neither of us heard Mistress Kimberly enter the bathroom. I don't know how long she was standing there, if she came in, left and returned again or if she even gave warning.

I do however remember the crack of the leather strap landing squarely across Justine's wet ass. The first volley took Justine's breath away. She gasped, but no sound came out. I retreated to the far corner and watched helplessly as Mistress Kimberly pulled Justine out of the shower by her hair and landed four additional strokes of the strap full force against her ass, which were just barely beginning to bring forth the red marks from the first four smacks.

"What in the fuck are the two of you thinking?" Mistress Kimberly screeched. She turned off the shower, reached in and pulled me out by my hair. As she dragged me out of the shower she landed four hard strokes of the strap against my soaked ass. I never felt as much pain in my life. My eyes instantly tear up. By the time I was out of the shower, I was face down on the floor and my ass was on fire from another volley from her strap.

"Get your fucking asses in the room now!" I have never seen Mistress Kimberly this angry before. "Stand in the middle of the room with your hands on top of your heads."

I never ran so fast in my life. I dare not touch my ass. We both obeyed her without wasting another moment. We knew what was about to come and there was no need in making it worse than it had to be.

Mistress Kimberly waste no time and lays into Justine's ass. The crack of the strap echoes throughout the room. I watch in fear as Justine struggled to hold her position as she cried out in pain.

"I send you in to shower and the two of you are fucking around."

She quickly turned her attention to my ass. I don't know how many strokes she gave me. All I know is that they came hard and fast. I was sobbing like a baby. All I wanted to do was runaway to some corner and rub my bottom. But I dare not move from my position.

Finally she stopped. "If tonight wasn't so important I would strap every inch of your bodies and not just your worthless asses." Mistress Kimberly points to the bed where our outfits are laid out. "Justy your outfit is at the head of the bed. I want the both of you dressed and in the living room in two minutes." Mistress Kimberly slammed the door behind her as she left.

There wasn't much to the outfits. They were identical with the exception that they were custom fitted to our exact measurements. We each had black rubber mini-skirts and bras and black patent leather knee high boots. We were not given panties to wear. The tight rubber mini-skirts insured that our raw asses reminded us of our misdeeds with every movement. It didn't matter if we moved or stood still, without panties the mini-skirts stuck firmly to our asses.

Mistress Kimberly took better care with her aim than I imagined. There was no sign that we had been strapped until we leaned forward and exposed our ass cheeks.

We didn't say a word, we just got dressed. I followed Justine into the living room. Justine walked to the center of the room and faced the sofa. She knelt down and rested her ass on her heels. Her hands laid flat on her knees and her back was straight, her head up and she looked forward. I took up the same position. My heels dug into my still throbbing ass, but I dare not move or make a sound.

A Special Night Out

I don't know how long we stayed in that position. Mistress Kimberly ignored us as she prepared herself. It seemed like we were there for hours. When Mistress Kimberly finally walked over to us, she looked hot. She was wearing a form fitting latex dress and patent leather fuck-me boots which came to her mid-thigh.

She walked around to the back of us and placed matching leather collars on us which had matching leashes attached to them. She picked up a red leather clutch purse and took hold of our leashes. "Up," she commanded us.

We quickly rose to our feet. My knees were stiff from kneeling so long. Mistress Kimberly led us out of the house by our leashes. She locked the door behind us. It seemed like a long walk down the driveway to her car. I don't think anyone saw us, but I really don't know. I wasn't doing much looking around. I was focused on getting to the car.

Mistress Kimberly opened the back door and Justine and I got in. The drive was quiet. Mistress Kimberly didn't even turn on the radio. We drove for about an hour. The restaurant was in the middle of nowhere. It was unlike any restaurant I have ever seen or been to. Everyone was dressed in fetish wear. Even the valet who parked Mistress Kimberly's car was a submissive dressed in leather bondage gear.

Mistress Kimberly led us in by our leashes. I wanted to look around, but I noticed that Justine kept her head down, so I did as she did and looked downward, glancing up just enough to see where I was going. Maybe if I didn't embarrass Mistress Kimberly or my Mistress any further tonight she will not tell my Mistress about our little indiscretion back at the house.

My Mistress walked up to Mistress Kimberly and Kissed her on her cheek and asked, "Is everything alright?" They were wearing matching outfits.

My heart stopped, I just knew she was going to say something.

"Everything is fine. I'm just nervous," Mistress Kimberly replied.

"Relax. She's back." My Mistress' eyes were actually sparkling. "She is excited to see you again. This is going to be so great."

"She hates me."

"Bullshit. She loves you."

"She loves you. She tolerates me."

"You know as well as I do she tolerates no one. You worry too much." Then I saw something that shocked me. Mistress smacked Mistress Kimberly playfully on her bottom. "Get your sexy ass in there."

Mistress took my leash from Mistress Kimberly and led me through the restaurant. When we got to the table Mistress tugged downward on my leash. I knelt next to the table and she tied my leash to a hook underneath the table. I assumed the same position as I was in back at Mistress Kimberly's house, except that I kept my head and eyes downward. Justine took the same position. My Mistress sat in the chair to my left, and Mistress Kimberly sat to the left of Justine.

There were two additional people already seated at the table. One I recognized as Master Adams. He was dressed in all black. It looks as if he lost weight. There was a woman seated next to him. I've never seen her before. She was gorgeous. She had long black hair which went down to the past her shoulders. She was wearing a chiffon red evening gown.

"Good evening Mistress." Mistress Kimberly spoke those words almost as she was a submissive herself.

The Mistress returned the greeting. "Hello Kimberly. There is no need for you to call me Mistress. Everyone seated at this table are all on equal footing."

"I feel as if I have so much to learn." Mistress Kimberly replied.

"That's why I'm here. I rearranged my schedule and we have the entire summer. Are you up for it?"

"Yes. I'm taking the entire summer off. So I have time."

"Are these the two you have chosen?"

Mistress Yvonne made the introductions. "Yes, these are our slaves." She motions down towards me. "This is one is mine. Her name is Sara." She motions towards Justine. "This one belongs to Mistress Kim, her name is Justine. Slaves say hello to Mistress Julie."

Justine and I answered in unison, "Hello Mistress Julie."

Mistress Julie looked at Mistress Yvonne and Mistress Kimberly. "Do you mind?"

Mistress Yvonne and Mistress Kimberly untied our leashes. They folded our leashes over and handed them to us. They motioned for us to walk over to Mistress Julie. We stood up, adjusted our skirts and walked over to Mistress Julie.

Mistress Julie stood up as we approached her. She walked over to a clearing in the dining area. We followed and stood facing her, still clutching our leashes. Mistress Julie circled around us, looking us over. She walked over to Justine and lifted her skirt up over her hips. She then did the same to me. Our shaven pussies and freshly strapped asses were totally exposed to everyone who cared to look. I do have to admit that the fresh air did feel good.

Mistress Julie pulled our skirts back down. "Very good, I see you taught them the basics." She motioned for us to return to our Mistress' sides. She returned to her seat. Master Adams stood up and held out her chair. We returned to our Mistresses sides and returned to our previous positions. Mistress Yvonne and Mistress Kimberly tied our leashes to the hooks on the table again.

Master Adams returned to his seat. "Mistress Julie will be completing your mentorship. I will stop by from time to time. You will spend the summer at the dungeon."

Mistress Yvonne asked, "When will we be expected to move in? We have a lease."

Mistress Julie answered, "I will expect you to be completely moved in by Monday. Bring any gear and toys you have. Everything else, including your clothing and food will be provided for you."

Master Adams added. "I will settle up your leases and place everything else in storage."

Mistress Kimberley asked, "Where will we live once school resumes?"

Mistress Julie answered in sort of a snooty way. "We will deal with that when the time comes. For now you are not to concern yourself with that."

That's easy for her to say. I like having a place to live while I go to school. I wasn't over joyed with the sudden news of my new living arrangements for the summer, but I did promise myself to my Mistress. I would do anything for her. I owe her that much.

Master Adams motioned for the waiter. "Now that that is settled let's celebrate." The waiter came over and was about to pass out the menus when Master Adams stopped him, "Champaign for the table and the seven course house specialty all around."

The waiter nodded and walked off. They made small talk while waiting for dinner. Most of it I don't remember, the rest is just boring. When the Champaign came, of course Justine and I didn't get glasses.

Master Adams made the toast, "To new beginnings."

After they drank, Mistress Yvonne turned to me and raised her glass, "To us and our new beginning." She took a sip and lowered the glass to my lips and I took a sip. Mistress Kimberly did the same with Justine.

It was at that moment I knew everything would be alright. I knew that no matter what happened this summer, my Mistress would take care of and protect me and Mistress Kimberly would do the same for Justine.

I have always trusted my Mistress. At that moment my trust and love deepened for her. I didn't mean to but I couldn't help it. I started to cry. Not like boo-hoo, but the tears were flowing.

Mistress Yvonne wiped my eyes. "Why are you crying mi amante?"

"I love you Mistress," I replied. I know it's really lame. But that's how I felt.

Mistress whispered in my ear, "Te amo también." Then she kissed me on my gently on my lips. "We'll talk about what happened to your ass when we get home."

"Yes Mistress." I love it when she does that. I get wet and weak in the knees.

When they started serving the meal they brought out those mini dinner trays that you use in bed for Justine and I. The legs were high enough that our legs were able to fit under them without us having to change positions.

I never had a seven course meal before. But they bring out each course of the meals one at a time. The waiter didn't serve Justine and I. Mistress Kimberly fed Justine from her plate and Mistress Yvonne fed me from her plate. The waiter did however take our plates after each course.

First they brought out appetizers, shrimp cocktails. They gave Mistress Kimberly and Mistress Yvonne extra plates with each course for Justine and me. We had vegetable soup and then a salad. That was followed by a lemon sorbet. It was a bit tangy for my taste, but of course I didn't say anything. We had some sort of fish. Then some sort of steak. It was small and round. As you can see I know nothing about fine dining. For desert we had peach cobbler topped with vanilla ice cream.

I don't think I was supposed to be looking around, but they were so involved in their conversation they didn't notice me. I hadn't really noticed when I first walked in, but every table had at least one submissive tied to it.

Most people would think that being chained to a table during dinner would be degrading. But it wasn't. I can't really explain it, but it was the second most special dinner I ever had with Mistress. The first being the night we first met. Since we met at a nightclub I don't think you can call it diner, especially since we didn't eat anything. But it was special to me.

Every course was more special than the last. It wasn't the food. I mean the food was excellent. But Mistress took such care preparing each course for me. She even cut the steak for me. I could tell that Mistress Julie was someone of importance to Mistress, but I felt as if I was the center of her universe. I just hope I make her feel the same about me.

The waiter came and removed my tray when the meal was done. Mistress stroked my hair and untied my leash. "Excuse me, but I feel like dancing." She stood up and I stood up as well. My knees were stiff, but I haven't danced with Mistress for a while. I enjoy dancing with her.

Master Adams stood up as Mistress escorted me to the dance floor. Mistress Kimberly and Justine followed, as did Master Adams and Mistress Julie.

Mistress held my leash while we danced, except when the band started playing a salsa. Mistress is an excellent salsa dancer. She has tried to teach me. I'm not bad for a white girl, but I struggle to keep up with Mistress. Every time she twirled me around my skirt would ride up my hips. Once again I was completely exposed, but I didn't care. At that moment Mistress only had eyes for me and I only had eyes for her.

I don't know when everyone else stopped dancing and started watching us. Most likely it was when my skirt first up rode up past

27

my hips. When the music stopped everyone started clapping and cheering. They formed a circle around us. It's hard to get Mistress to blush, but I swear she turned two shades of red. Her face was almost as red as my ass when Mistress Kimberly finished with me.

We danced and socialized for about another three hours. Justine and I didn't do much socializing, but we did have a great time dancing. When it was time to leave we left together. Master Adams paid for everything.

As we waited for the valet to bring our cars around Mistress Julie tied up some loose ends. "I will send someone around to pick up Justine and Sara over the weekend. I will expect Kimberly and you Monday morning for breakfast, and we will get started."

Mistress Yvonne asked, "What day and what time should we have them ready?"

"Just have them ready. It can be anytime as soon as tomorrow morning. It depends on when I can arrange it. I will contact you before I have them picked up."

Mistress Kimberly asked, "So should Yvonne and I be ready to go with them?"

"No, I'm just sending someone to pick them up and get them settled in." Mistress Julie could see the stress in Kimberly's face. "I promise nothing will happen to them. No one will be permitted to touch them without your expressed permission."

That was a relief to hear. When our cars came around Master Adams tipped the valets for each car. Of course I went home with my Mistress. Before I got into the car Mistress removed my skirt and folded it up and placed it in the back seat. She sat me in the front seat. No one seemed to even notice me standing there butt-naked and ass out. It was normal to them, I guess.

I knew I was in for it once I got home but I didn't care. I was more concerned about what the summer had for me. We didn't talk on the way home. It wasn't that Mistress was angry with me. She rarely talks in the car. Most times we don't even play the radio.

When we pulled up in the parking lot things got very stressful for me. I suddenly remembered I was bare ass and it was quite a walk to our apartment. It was half past mid-night, but there were still people passing by on the street. What if someone pulled up in the parking lot or passed us in the hall.

I guess it really didn't matter, since we will be leaving by this weekend. But it would be hard to explain. Of course Mistress took her time while escorting me across the parking lot and to our door.

When we got to our door Mistress hung my skirt on Master Craig's door knob. I still can't get use to calling him Master. But I have learned to respect him as a Master. Mistress opened the door and led me in.

Mistress closed and locked the door behind us. "So explain to me why Mistress Kim felt she needed to strap your ass?"

"Mistress Kimberly told Justine and me to shower. She came in and caught us together and she strapped us, because we were wasting time when we should have been getting ready for tonight."

Mistress examined my ass. "By all rights I should give you another strapping. But it looks as if Mistress Kim has made her point."

"Thank you Mistress." Usually it wouldn't matter how well Mistress Kimberly strapped my ass, I would be in for another round by Mistress. But tonight maybe the last time we are together this weekend, I think she just wanted to end the evening on a positive note.

"Get undressed and prepare for bed."

"Yes Mistress." I went into our room, removed my boots and bra. I put them away. I went to the foot of our bed and knelt there holding my leash out for Mistress.

I heard a knock at the door. I recognized the voice as Master Craig. I don't know what they were talking about. I really couldn't make it out. They spoke for about an hour, before he left. I held my position the entire time. I was so proud of myself.

29

When Mistress came into our room she was carrying my skirt. She placed it the dresser. She undressed and took my leash and led me into our bed.

I could tell she had been crying. "Is everything alright Mistress?"

Mistress never answered me. She released my leash, pushed me down onto my back, and pulled me to her by my legs. She knelt on the bed, pulled my legs over her shoulders, lifted me up by my hips and buried her face between my legs.

Mistress has always been a very attentive lover, but tonight was different. It was as if we were making love for the first time and the last. It was as if there was no one else in her world but me. She was so intense I could barely breathe. You know how when you get so wet and excited that thick creamy cum builds up inside you, I saw it all over Mistress' face when she looked up. She looked so hot.

She crawled up between my legs and gave me the deepest kiss ever. I made sure to kiss every drop of my juices off her face. She then crawled up and sat on my face. Her pussy was just as wet and slimy as mine. I enjoyed lapping up every drop.

I know every inch of Mistress' body, especially where her special spot was. I gripped her hips and focused all of my efforts on her special spot. She went wild. The more she struggled the more I tightened my grip. I didn't stop until she collapsed from exhaustion. I gave Mistress multiple orgasms.

When I finally released her we kissed and she held me tight all night long.

Mistress whispered in my ear, "I want you to know that no matter what I love you."

"I love you too Mistress. I trust you."

Mistress started crying, "You don't have to go through with this. I will still be with you if you don't want to do this?"

For the first time this evening I looked Mistress in her eyes. This time it was me drying her eyes. "Everyone keeps thinking I don't

30

know what I'm doing. I have looked into this lifestyle. When I gave myself to you, I knew what I was doing. I want 24/7 with you. I know what that means. Everything I am, I pledge to you, my Mistress."

"Why? You are smart and beautiful. You can do or be anything you want. Why are you willing to do this for me?"

"You are my Mistress. Will you allow me to be anything less than my best?"

"No."

"Will you allow any harm to come to me?"

"No."

"That's why. I can trust you not only with my safety, but with who I am and who I will become."

We didn't talk again that night. Mistress did however wake me several times to make love. We didn't get out of bed until well past noon the next morning. It was then that I realized that Mistress was more nervous than I. I really don't know why that was.

From where I am, she has the easy part. She gets to spank, punish and use me anyway she wishes. I have to keep her interested and keep the other sluts away from her. I mean, when you think about it, she picked me out of a crowd. She is so hot she can have any girl she want, or guy for that matter if she so desired. Where am I going to find another Mistress like her?

Anticipation

It was too late for breakfast when we finally got up, so I made tacos. Not real tacos I just fried corn tortillas into hard shells and ground beef with the seasoning you get out of the packet. I did however make real lemonade, with real lemons. I squeezed them with my own hands.

Mistress Yvonne and I didn't bother getting fully dressed when we got up. I put on an old white cotton tee shirt, with a bear on it. It had a Russian website on it. I got it at one of those discount stores. I bought it because I like bears. I also put on a cute pair of panties I have. They were a lavender pink string bikini cut type. I like them because they have two latches in the front, which make it sort of fun to take off. When I stood up the tee shirt barely covered my ass. It was really nothing fancy. To my surprise the strap marks on my ass had faded away. I was sure I would have them for several days. I guess she didn't strap us all that hard after all.

Mistress Yvonne wore a lacy pair of powder blue panties and a plan white tee shirt. Her tee shirt was a bit longer than mine. It came down about mid-thigh. I sort of wish it was a bit shorter. I like my Mistress' thighs.

I really enjoy watching Mistress eat my tacos. She really gets into it. Normally she is so proper when she eats. She says she likes that I lightly fry the corn tortilla and fold them over. I add the beef and cheese while the shells are still warm. The shell melts the cheese into the beef. I add the taco sauce, lettuce and top with diced tomatoes. Like I said they are really nothing special, but watching Mistress you would think they were from a five star restaurant.

After lunch we cleaned up. We didn't talk much. It wasn't like a dead silence. It was more like sporadic small talk. I don't know who was more nervous, Mistress Yvonne or myself. I guess the reality was beginning to set in for me.

I walked into our room. I intended to get dressed, but I found myself staring out the window. Mistress came in and sort of watched me from across the room. I'm almost afraid to go outside. I have wild images of a van pulling up and grabbing me off the street. Part of me is excited, but at the same time it's really scary. I don't know what to expect. I don't think Mistress knows what to expect either.

I don't know when Mistress picked up the camcorder. I looked over and noticed she was filming me. I don't know why, I mean I really didn't think about it, I walked over to the bed and sat on it. As Mistress filmed me I put on a show for her. It was sort of fun. I felt naughty.

I ran my hands all over my body. I'm not the seductive type, but I felt really sexy. I didn't really notice the camera. I only saw my Mistress. I leaned back and rubbed my tummy under the tee shirt. Mistress likes my tummy. I know that's a dumb thing to call it, but Mistress refers to my stomach as my tummy.

I unfastened one side of my panties and let one side fall down. I then slowly unfastened the other side and pulled my panties between my legs and dropped them on the bed.

I am not what you would call booty-licious. I have sort of a narrow ass. It's not flat, but it's really nothing special. For some strange reason Mistress likes it. So I did my best to be seductive and stuck my ass out and spread my cheeks slightly apart. I could feel the cool breeze across my open asshole.

The more she filmed the more I got into it. I even found myself masturbating for Mistress. At first I just knelt there and slowly masturbated and rubbed my tits occasionally. I could tell I was turning Mistress on, so I leaned back and spread my legs about shoulder length apart. I lifted my ass forward to give Mistress a better view.

After a few minutes Mistress turned off the camcorder and set it down. She pulled off her tee shirt and stepped out of her panties.

33

She walked over to the side of the bed and pulled me to her by my ponytails. It was the wettest sloppiest kiss I ever received from Mistress. I loved it. It was warm and sloppy wet.

Mistress forced me back onto the bed, never once taking a breath. She slipped two fingers deep inside me and began finger fucking me into frenzy. It wasn't long until I was near orgasm. Right when I was about to cum, Mistress stopped. She just stopped!

Mistress pinned my hands up over my head. She moved her pussy over my face and sat on my face. She used her knees to keep my arms pinned down. I have never been so frustrated before. It was driving me crazy. The more I ate Mistress' pussy the more frustrated I became. I was thrashing about like a fish out of water. All I wanted to do was to cum, but I couldn't.

I tried concentrating on Mistress' pussy. I forced my tongue as far inside Mistress as I could. I was on a mission to make her cum. The sooner Mistress cum the sooner I would be allowed to cum. Mistress leaned back and pulled my knees up and in front of her. She held me in place by my ankles. I could feel the cool air enter my wet pussy as my pussy lips spread apart.

This position forced her pussy tighter onto my face. I so needed to cum. I was about to lose my mind. Finally Mistress released her juices into my mouth. I could feel her pussy walls pulsate against my lashing tongue.

Mistress climbed off me, "Don't you dare touch yourself. I don't want you to cum."

"Mistress, please." I was desperate.

Mistress didn't answer. She got up and went into the bathroom and started dressing. I laid there for a few minutes and composed myself. I got up and I also started to dress.

We had planned to pack, but we didn't know what we would need to take with us. I have like two collars and leashes that Mistress gave me, not counting the one I wore last night. I have a few outfits Mistress likes. It took us all of twenty minutes to pack.

We finally got up enough courage to go out jogging. We only put in about three miles, but it broke up the day and relieved a bit of my frustration. About an hour after we returned home, Mistress received a call. She took it in the bedroom, so I don't know what was said.

About thirty minutes later Mistress came back into the living room. She was carrying my yellow sundress and a pair of my sandals. "Take everything off, including your panties and bra and put these on."

"Yes Mistress." I quickly undressed and took the sundress and sandals from Mistress and put them on. I picked up the clothing I had just stepped out of and quickly took them into the bathroom and placed them in the hamper and returned to the living room.

Mistress Yvonne hadn't moved. "They will be here around ten o'clock to pick you up. You can still change your mind if you want."

"I won't lie. I am nervous and a bit scared, but I really want to do this. I want this to be more than just a part of my life. I want to be yours 24/7."

"Mistress Julie is faxing me an agreement for you to sign before they pick you up tonight. It will basically say that you agree to do this of your own free will and you are free to leave at any time."

"As long as you are there I will be alright. I don't know if I would like to be a pet, like Justine. But I definitely want to be in a Total Power Exchange relationship. Justine told me a little about it and I think that is what I want."

Mistress Yvonne sat down on the sofa. "I want this because I want to do more, but I want to do it right. I don't want to hurt you. Sometimes I feel guilty as if I'm taking advantage of you."

I knelt next to Mistress and placed my head on her lap and looked up at her. "You are definitely not taking advantage of me. I want more. I want it all. I trust you. I love you."

Mistress started stroking my hair. "I love you too. When I met you, you were innocent about this lifestyle and I feel as if I just threw you into it."

"I admit I knew nothing about this lifestyle before I met you. But I wasn't alive until I met you. If it wasn't for you I would still be living a lie." I paused for a moment. I almost didn't ask, but I just had to ask. "Who are Mistress Julie, Master Adams and Master Craig to you?"

Mistress stopped stroking my hair and held my hands. "Mistress Julie is Kim and my mentor. She is guiding us in learning what we need to know."

"So she tells you the rules?"

"Yes and no. There are really no rules except for safety and consent. We decide what we want to do and how. She just guides us. Master Adams is actually Mistress Julie's husband and her Master, as far as I can tell. I'm really not sure how their relationship works. Master Craig is a friend and confidant of mine. When things get too rough he is there to talk me through them. He is also a good friend of Master Adams and Mistress Julie."

"How do you know Mistress Kimberly? If it's none of my business just say so, I will understand."

"We dated for about a week. We figured out we were better as friends. Our personalities were too much alike to continue dating. We kept trying to dominate each other." She sighed slightly. "Our current relationship is somewhat like Justine and yours."

"Sort of like a friends with benefits thing?"

I could tell by Mistress' expression I caught her off guard. "Sort of I guess."

"That's fine with me. I don't see that as cheating. I know it may sound strange, but as long as it's just our small group it's sort of like our own family. Like Mistress Kimberly and you are in charge of Justine and me. I see you as being in charge of all of us."

"I think you think too much. Kim and Justine are coming over for dinner. We are going to order pizza. For now I just want to sit here quietly with you."

I didn't say another word. I went and got a blanket, curled up next to Mistress and wrapped the blanket around us. I'm not sure but I think we both dozed off for about ten minutes.

About an hour and a half later Mistress Kimberly and Justine walked in carrying two pizzas and two of bottles of red wine. Justine was also wearing only a yellow sundress and sandals. I could tell that she wasn't wearing a bra and when she sat on the ground next to the sofa I could see she wasn't wearing any panties.

I got up to sit on the ground next to Justine, Mistress pointed towards the kitchen. "Go and get four glasses for us."

"Yes Mistress." We don't have those fancy wine glasses, so I brought back four glasses with mismatch designs. I also brought four plates. I heard the fax machine in our bedroom start up. I returned and set the glasses and plates on the coffee table next to the pizza and bottles of wine.

Justine walked out of our room carrying some papers. She handed them to Mistress Yvonne. "It looks like there are two sets. One set with my name and the other with Sara's name on it."

Mistress looked them over for a moment. Mistress Kimberly walked over and read them as well. After they finished looking the papers over Mistress sorted the papers into two stacks. She handed one to me and another to Justine. "I'll go get a couple of pens. You need to read these over and sign them."

It was two pages long each. Basically it said we were staying at the dungeon of our own free will and that we could leave at any time and that we were in good health. When Mistress returned we signed the agreements. I guess that's what you could call them. Mistress Kimberly set the signed agreements on the sofa.

We sat around the coffee table, ate pizza, drank wine and talked. I don't recall what we talked about. It was mainly small talk. I do know that we didn't speak about what lay ahead of us. Everyone was a bit nervous I suspect.

About twenty minutes after we finished eating there was a knock at the door. Everyone froze. You could hear a pin drop. An even louder knock followed.

Mistress Yvonne called out, "Who is it?"

A male voice responded from the other side of the door. "We are here to pick up a Sara McNeil and Justine Baker."

"We'll be with you in a minute", Mistress Kimberly responded.

Mistress Yvonne walked over and opened the door. Four incredibly buffed black men entered. They were carrying two of those metal pet cages. You know the ones you would put a dog in. They appeared to be specially made. The metals were thicker and they looked heavy. They set the cages down in the middle of the room. One of the men asked, "Who is Justine and who is Sara."

Justine raised her hand, "I'm, Justine."

I raised my hand as well, "I'm Sara."

He looked us over and then ordered, "Get undressed and get into the cages. We have eight others to pick up tonight."

Suddenly it was real. This was really going to happen. I could feel the butterflies in my stomach as I pulled the dress up over my head. I stepped out of my sandals. I folded my dress and placed it on the sofa next to Justine's. I looked over at the cages. Suddenly they didn't look as big as when they first bought them in. "I don't think we will fit."

"You will fit", he replied. "Crawl in head first." He unlashed the door to the cages.

We knelt down and crawled in. It was snug, but we fit just fine.

"Do you have the agreements?" I heard one of the men ask.

"Yeah, here" Mistress Kimberly replied.

"Thanks, you'll have copies on Monday" I heard him reply.

They lifted up the cages and carried us out the door. It was cold out. The cold night air cut through me to the bone. They opened the rear of the van door and slid us in with the other cages. All of the other cages were empty except for two of them. The girls in the other two cages were completely nude as well. They tied down our cages and then closed the door. When all of the men got into the van we drove off. I was never so grateful for a heater in my entire life.

No one talked, not even the men. No one said we couldn't talk, but I guess we were just too nervous and what would we talk about anyways. It was a bit bumpy, but if I laid down flat it was not so bad. We drove for about an hour. At least that is what it felt like.

When the van stopped two men got out. They returned about ten minutes later and loaded another caged girl into the van. I had a passing thought at that moment. If they were to be pulled over by the police, how would they explain a van full of naked caged girls? I had to catch myself; I almost started laughing out loud.

They drove around all night collecting girls. They collected a dozen of us and stacked our cages two high with two rows three deep. I drifted off to sleep a few times, but I really didn't get much rest. I don't think any of us did.

Orientation

It was dawn before we arrived at the dungeon. When the van stopped all of the men got out. I could hear them lock the doors. It must have been at least twenty minutes before someone came out. I couldn't see who it was, but someone got in and drove the van around to the back loading area.

As soon as we finished backing up to the dock the rear doors flung open. A team of men dressed in leather harnesses unloaded us from the van and onto the dock. We were treated as cargo. They treated us with care, but they never said anything to us and they just left us there in the cold.

They brought out smaller cages and set one in front of each of us. The cages were made of that see through acrylic. It had a hole in the front and one in the back. The one in the back was a bit higher than the one in the front. It also had four metal rings near the top of the cage. Two rings on each side. One near the front and one near the back. It had latches on the left side, looking out at it from my cage. They unlatched the acrylic cages and opened them like a chest, one at a time.

They opened our cages and allowed us to get out and stretch for a few minutes. Then one of the men spoke, "You are to get into the examination cages in front of you. Stick your head out the front hole and tuck your knees under to your chest."

One of the girls responded, "I don't think we will fit." She had a strong British accent. She was a cute brunette. She was on the tall side about 5 feet 10 inches. But she was very slender.

"You will fit," the man responded. "When your Masters and Mistresses first signed you up they sent in all of your measurements. Everything here has been custom fitted for each of you."

We each got into the cage with our name on it and they closed us in and locked the latches closed. It was a snug fit, but we did fit. I hadn't noticed before but the holes for our necks were padded. My ass pressed firmly against the rear of the cage. The rear hole left my pussy and ass completely exposed.

A group of men came out, two for each cage. Each was carrying a metal pole. They slid a metal pole through the rings on the cages. One man stood in the front while another stood to the rear. They picked us up by the poles. They placed the poles on their shoulders and marched us inside.

We entered a medical room. It had six large metal exam tables. They placed three cages side by side on four of the tables. A male doctor entered the room. He was followed by four nurse, two men and two women.

Each of the nurses walked over to the far corner and took an exam cart. They wheeled a cart next to each of our tables and stood next to the table. A male nurse stood next to the table I was on. Justine and the British girl were also on the same table I was on.

The doctor stood in front of us. "This will be your initial exam. You have been arranged on the tables according to your rooming arrangements. You have also been assigned a nurse, if you have any medical needs or concerns you will contact your assigned nurse. My name is Doctor Elkin. Your exams will begin now and then you will be led to your rooms where you can get dressed."

I hear the snapping of surgical gloves. Our nurse walked to the front of us and introduced himself. "Good morning ladies. My name is Matt. I need each of you to open wide so I can check your throats."

I hate those wooden tongue depressors. They always make me gag. And good old Matt stuck it way down my throat. He took his time inspecting my throat. Drool was flowing from my mouth by the time he was done. I thought I was going to choke on my own spit. He went on to Justine, who was next to me. By the time he got to the British girl I heard one of the girls on the table in front of me let out a deep groan. I looked up and her nurse had her finger deep in the poor girl's ass hole. I was not looking forward to that. Matt had huge hands.

Matt removed his glove and walked over to the cart and wheeled it behind us. I could hear him putting on new gloves. He started by spreading my pussy lips apart with his one hand and probing me with one and then two fingers from his free hand. His lubed fingers slid in and out of me with ease as he spread me open and probed around. He then slid his fingers into my ass. I was helpless. The examination cage held me in place.

He removed his gloves and replaced them with new ones. He performed the same exam on Justine and the British girl. He then inserted rectal thermometers into each of us. "I will schedule complete examinations for each of you by the end of the week."

"What is the purpose of this?" Justine asked.

"Think of this as a meet and greet. I'm just giving you a quick once over." Matt opened our cages and helped us out one by one.

It felt good to finally be out of that contraption.

Doctor Elkin clapped his hands to get out attention. "Your nurses will escort you to your dorms where you will find clothes. In the future you will not be confined inside of the exam cages unless you put up a struggle." He then left the room.

Matt smiles, "Now that we are acquainted, follow me ladies." He led us through the dungeon to a section I never saw before. He unlocked the door to our room. "Your names are on your beds. Put on your training collars. You will wear them at all times. They have a security chip in them that will automatically open any door you have access to without you having to use a key, including your dorm room. Each of you will share a third of the closet space and you have a dresser and night stand by each of your beds. The phone connects you to the operator for now. When your Mistresses arrive it will connect you to their room, unless they are out and then it will connect to the operator. Someone will be around to check on you in about 15 minutes. Put on the clothes which are laid out on your beds."

He left before any of us could ask any questions. I immediately found my bed and started dressing. Justine on the other hand found it more important to make introductions. She walked up to the British girl, "Hello, my name is Justine and this is Sara." She pointed to me, "and you are?"

The British girl looked a bit surprised but answered almost immediately. "I'm Elyse. I guess we're to be new mates."

Justine started looking around as Elyse and I dressed. There wasn't much to see. We had the main room with our beds, a vanity room with three vanity stations, a wash room with an extremely large bath tub with three shower attachments, a room with a toilet and another area with three wash basins. It was a good size room. We did have a mini fridge and television with a DVD player in the main room.

Justine finally got around to getting dressed. They didn't give us mush to wear. We had our collars, bra, panties, shoes, socks and a blue prison dress. It was an extremely ugly dress. There was nothing else in the closet or in our dressers.

After we got dressed we just sort of sat on our beds. So I figured I would get to know Elyse. "What part of England are you from Elyse?"

"I'm from Brentwood, Essex. It's about 48 kilometers from London."

Justine asked, "So why did you come to the America?"

Elyse answered, "My dad's job transferred him to America and we just stayed."

"Do you miss England?"

"Yeah, me family is there. But we have been back a few times for holiday. I may go back someday for good."

"So how long have you been a submissive?"

"As long as I can remember, I just recently found out that there were others like me."

I asked "How did you meet your Mistress, or Master?"

Elyse actually started to blush. I could see she was actually in love. "I met my Mistress at a meet and greet. I found this BDSM group that meet once a month. It's just a gathering there is no play. She just walked up to me and introduced herself. After speaking with her five minutes I knew she was the one for me."

Just when the conversation was getting good the phone rang. Justine answered it. "Hello." She listened intensely for a few minutes. "Okay". And then she hung up the phone. "They want us to come down to breakfast."

"Is someone coming to collect us?" Elyse asked.

It took Justine a moment to process what Elyse said. "No, it's just down the hall and to the left. They want us there in five minutes."

"What if we make a wrong turn and get lost?" I asked. "They really should send someone to show us the way."

Justine replied, "It's just down the hall and to the left. How are we going to get lost?" She shook her head and smiled at me. "You can hold my hand so you don't wander off, if you like."

Justine can be a bitch at times. But I guess I had it coming. It was a silly thing to say.

Our First Breakfast

We got up and walked to breakfast. There was no lock on the door. It locked and unlocked automatically. We just sort of followed the crowd. I only remember seeing twelve girls, but there were six male subs also headed to breakfast. I guess they came in on another van.

They made everyone line up at the door. Justine Elyse and I were pulled aside and told to wait until everyone else were lead in. The setup was similar to the restaurant we went to the other evening. One by one everyone was lead to a table and leashed to an eye hook on one of the legs of the table.

After about ten minutes they lead Justine Elyse and I into the dining room. The tables in the center of the room where the other subs were leashed were round tables with white table cloths and fresh flowers as a center piece. There was a long table, with a white table cloth draped over it, in the back of the room. It was sort of a staging area for the servers I guess. The waiters and waitresses were lined up along the far wall as you enter the dining room.

We were lead to the long table in the front of the dining room. It had a long white table cloth which went all the way down to the floor. The table cloths on the other tables only went about half way down to the floor. The head table was adorned with flowers, candles and assorted fruit arrangements.

Behind the head table there six wooded posts, with large heavy steel rings bolted to the front of the posts. There were three metal rings on each post, one near the bottom, one near the center and one near the top. As you walked towards the head table there were three posts to the right of the center seat, which was the only chair with a high wooden back to it, with plush red leather padding on the back and seat. There was another set of three posts to the left.

We were lead to the set of posts to the left. We were leashed to the lower metal rings. I was on the post closest to the center, Justine was leashed to the center post and Elyse was leashed to the end leash. It was sort of cool. Because we were elevated, we could see out across the entire dining room. I don't know why we were placed up front. I didn't think to ask.

We were left in the dining room alone for about five minutes. Well, we weren't totally alone. The service staff was still lined up along the wall. But they didn't move or look around. They were almost like statues.

I guess the fact that we were on display didn't seem to bother Justine and Elyse. I mean, I knew we will always be on display, but do we have to eat with everyone looking at us? That can be a lot of pressure. Everyone was just staring at us.

I leaned over to Justine and asked, "So are these our perches or do they rotate us?"

Justine just shrugged her shoulders.

Elyse leaned over, "For as long as our Mistresses hold their positions, these are our posts."

"How do you know so much?"

"My Mistress told me." Elyse leaned in closer, looked around and whispered, "Our Mistresses are being groomed to take this over. Mater Adams and Mistress Julie own dungeons all over the world."

Justine's face lit up, "So we are the top bitches here?"

Elyse sat back, "Don't let it go to your head. We're still submissive."

Justine flashed her wicked smile, "I think I'm going to like it here."

Finally an older man with a greying mustache, no beard, entered in from the kitchen door which was located at the rear of the dining room. He was wearing one of those white chef uniforms and one of those stupid looking chef hats. I guess he was the head chef or something like that. He spoke loudly. "Normally your Masters or Mistresses would serve you from the food we bring to their tables. But for today we will serve you. You are not to start eating until

Master Adams and Mistress Julie arrives and gives you permission."

I guess he wasn't much of a conversationalist. He abruptly turned and quickly walked back into the kitchen. As soon as the door swung shut the staff came to life. They started by placing plates and glasses in front of us. I did notice that a few subs had two bowls placed in front of them. I figured they were like pets or something. I was surprised that Justine didn't have bowls placed in front of her. I thought she was a cat or rabbit or some type of fuzzy pet.

It seemed a bit odd, but they took our empty plates and bowls and replaced them with full plates and bowls. I mean why set out empty plates and not use them?

Anyway, the food smelled good. We had scrambled eggs, beacon, breakfast potatoes and fresh fruit. We were served orange juice and milk along with a glass of water.

Master Adams and Mistress Julie didn't keep us waiting. As soon as the last plate was served they entered. Master Adams came up to the front and spoke, "I hope the trip over wasn't too stressful. For the rest of the day you will have free run of the mansion. You are free to look around, both inside and out. Get to know each other, especially your roommates. You will be together for a while."

Mistress Julie continued, "Tomorrow your Masters and Mistresses will have all arrived, your training officially being then. You will be called in for a more complete exam later today. Other than that you are on free time. Enjoy your breakfast."

They left the dining room. When the door closed behind them a low hum of voices mixed with silverware clicking on the plates filled the room. The subs with the bowls food was cut up into bit sized pieces and their other dish was filled with water or milk. They didn't have juice.

I couldn't resist. I turned to Justine, "I thought you were a gerbil or something? Why didn't they give you bowls to eat from?"

I could tell from her voice that I got to her. "I was never a gerbil", She replied. "I was a kitten, and a damn sexy one at that. It really wasn't working for us. We are still doing the twenty four seven thing, I am just a sub. I think I look good in my kitten suit but Mistress couldn't get into it."

Elyse asked, "Did you like being a kitten?"

Justine nodded, "Yeah, I liked it. But it was too much all of the time. We still role play at times and she still takes me to the furry conventions."

Elyse responded, "So you're a furry. That's why the whole pet thing didn't work for you. Furries tend to walk around and do things other than what a pet would."

Justine got her she-devil look on her face. "Yeah, Mistress wanted me to play with yarn and stuff while she was off doing other things. I wanted to interact more with her."

"So you're a neko?"

Justine actually lit up, "Yeah."

I never knew any of this about her. "What in the hell is a furry convention? And what the fuck is a neko?" I was totally lost.

I could see a panic wash over Justine's face. It was almost as if she forgot I was there. I thought she was going to become sick.

I continued, "I'm not judging you. I knew you were into the twenty four seven power transfer thing. So am I. I would love to live in a full out relationship like that. I also knew you were a pet, but I never heard of a furry or a neko."

Elyse jumped in after a few minutes of silence. "A pet is someone, not always a submissive, whose identity either in a twenty four seven relationship or in play is that of a pet, such as a dog or a cat. A furry is a little more involved. Furries tend to walk around on two legs, some even talk, but most usually don't. Furries tend to have a mixture of human personalities along with the animal they personify. The furry can be anything such as a fox, dog or anything the furry can imagine it wants to be. Neko is Japanese for cat. So Justine is a cat-girl."

"I think I understand." I wasn't a hundred percent sure for what she was talking about, but I figured I will find out more from Justine later.

Justine looked up at me, "You are not like all freaked out by this?"

"Why would I be freaked out? I'm sitting here chained to a beam eating in a room full of other people chained to table legs and eating from the floor." I took hold of her hand, "Every since I met Mistress, nothing surprises me anymore."

Justine smiled a sigh of relief.

Elyse asked, "What is your neko name?"

"Kazumi, it means harmonious beauty."

That name totally fit her. Looking at Justine I could see Kazumi in her. Being a neko and a furry fits her a lot better than just being a pet.

Breakfast was pretty good. Everything was fresh. They even brought out fresh assorted melon balls. It almost felt like a last meal. I mean, I hate watermelon and I love cantaloupe. I was served only cantaloupe. Justine even had a scoop of cottage cheese on top of her melon balls. I don't hate cottage cheese, but it isn't my favorite food. Elyse had red Jell-O.

It seemed like everyone had something special on their plates. It was as if they were apologizing to us in advanced for what was to come. I tried not to think about it too much. No one else seemed to be concerned. Maybe I do over think things. After breakfast they unleashed us and sent us back to our rooms to freshen up and then the rest of the day would be ours.

Their Babe Gurl

When we got back to our room, all I wanted to do was sleep. So far things have been very tame, which makes me nervous. I felt grimy so I headed straight for the shower. The problem was that Justine and Elyse had the same idea. The three of us stood staring at the shower motionless.

Justine broke the silence, "Well we can't just stand here. Who is going to shower first?"

Elyse pointed at the shower, "There are three shower heads obviously they meant for us to shower at the same time. Just look at how huge the tub is."

They started undressing. I went back into the main room. "I'm going to sleep. I can't keep my eyes open." I flopped face down on the bed. "What the fuck?" I don't know how long I was lying down. I was just feeling myself drift off when Justine had my dress up over my head and Elyse had my panties past my knees and flung them across the room. I immediately sat up to protest. Before I could say anything Justine had my bra off and Elyse yanked me to my feet and was dragging me to the bathroom.

Elyse pulled me into the tub and turned on the shower heads. "We took a vote and we decided that no one in this room will ever go to bed funky, even if the others have to give them a sponge bath."

The warm water was refreshing. I wanted to protest, but those luffas felt so relaxing on my back and stomach. I realized just how sadistic Elyse can be when she slowly worked a soapy luffa inside of my pussy by slowly twisting it back and forth until it was about half ways inside me. She started moving it in and out slowly, while twisting it. It hurt like hell, but it was something erotic about it. I sure in hell didn't want her to stop.

Elyse spoke to Justine as if I wasn't there. "You are right. She is a little slut."

Justine leaned close to me so that her breasts were pressed firm against my back. She placed her head on my shoulder as if to whisper in my ear. She pulled my head back by my hair. The water poured down my face as she answered, "She plays little Miss Innocent, but she will fuck you into a comma."

"She sure doesn't put up much of a fight. I thought for sure she would be freaking out by now."

"She is a fucking perfect submissive. She's a natural. It is as if she was born to be used, abused and humiliated."

"When her Mistress isn't using her, maybe we can teach her some new tricks?" Before I could respond Elyse pulled the luffa out of me and rubbed it against my erect and exposed clit. It was almost too much to take. She barely touched me, but it sent little electric shockwaves throughout my body.

Justine patted me lightly on my bottom. "We need a name for her."

"I have a name, Sara." I replied as dignified as I could, while trying not to swallow too much water.

Elyse placed her left index finger against my lips. "Shush baby girl, the grownups are talking.

Justine licked my ear and released her grip on my hair. "I like it. We will call her Babe Gurl. We can spell it B-A-B-E G-U-R-L."

"I'm not a baby." I don't know why I said that, but I did. So deal with it. It was all that I could think of.

Elyse can be a patronizing bitch when she want to, "Awe how cute. I think it fits her perfectly. Babe Gurl it is." Elyse positioned her face inches from mine. She was so close we were almost kissing as she spoke. "Maybe we can convince her Mistress to tattoo it across her sweet little ass."

Elyse leaned forward. I braced myself for a kiss that never came. She pulled me closer and embraced Justine in a long passionate kiss. It was almost as if I wasn't even there.

Elyse and Justine kissed me gently as they slowly knelt down. Elyse lifted my right leg and guided it over her shoulder. Elyse's tongue invaded my pussy as Justine's tongue pierced my clinching asshole.

I didn't even know Elyse and already she was eating me out with Justine, like I was some sort of slut sandwich. I guess I could have protested, but they have two wicked tongues and Justine was just a nasty ass bitch who knew how to get me off.

They didn't allow me to cum. They took me right to the edge and then shut off the shower and got out of the tub. I moved my hand between my legs. I felt a sharp smack across my wet ass. Damn that hurt.

Justine snapped at me, "Don't you dare. You don't cum without our permission."

"Ma'am may I please cum?" I quivered.

Elyse delivered an equally stinging smack across my other cheek. "Permission denied. Neither one of us are your Mistress."

"Then what the fuck are you?" I was about to explode.

Justine helped me out of the tub and started drying me off with a large soft towel. "We're your big sisters, who only want what is best for you."

"Then sisters may I please cum?" I so needed to cum.

Elyse wiped her fingers across my pussy. She held up her fingers and spread them apart slowly. The slim dripping from my cunt clung between her finger tips, "It looks as if you are already done."

How embarrassing. She licked her fingers clean and then went back for more. She knelt between my legs and licked me clean as Justine dried me off with the towel. I in turn dried them off.

Although I was refreshed, I was still quite sleepy. I don't know how we all fit, but we crawled into one bed and fell asleep. We didn't bother to dress or get under the covers.

We slept until they rang us for lunch. Lunch was light. I just had soup and salad. No one spoke much we still weren't sure what to expect. I remember when we were here for Justine's collaring a little while back. But I doubt it will be anything like that.

It was a beautiful day so after lunch we decided to go swimming. The problem was that we didn't have bathing suits. We figured we would just sit by the pool and get a little sun. When we got out there it seems that everyone else had the same idea. Everyone was naked laying out sunning themselves and skinny dipping.

Justine, Elyse and I found a group of those long reclaimable patio chairs next to the Jacuzzi. Justine wasted no time in stripping, setting her clothes on the patio table next to us. Elyse and I weren't so enthusiastic but eventually we stripped as well. It felt odd being the only ones dressed.

Elyse joined Justine in the pool. I closed my eyes for a bit as I laid back. I wasn't sleepy or anything. I didn't have my shades and the sun was glaring in my eyes. I wanted to work on my tan a bit. I wasn't sure when I would get another chance. Of course I didn't have sun block and I burn almost instantly. So after a few minutes I rolled over onto my stomach.

As soon as I got comfortable I felt someone dripping on me. I waited for Justine or Elyse to say something. But no one spoke. They just stood there dripping on me. "We didn't bring towels, so you will just have to drip back to the room to dry off." I figured they wanted me to go get it for them.

I almost had a heart attack when this deep rich South African male voice responded. "Etiquette dictates that we at least know each other's names before such intimates."

I turned over so fast I almost rolled out of my chair. I crossed my legs and covered up as best I could. I would like to tell you that the first thing I noticed was this incredibly handsome man with the darkest and smoothest skin I have ever seen in my life. It was almost like silk. He was fit and trim, muscular, but not gross like a body builder. And he had an eight-pack. I never knew you could get an eight-pack. His eyes were so warm and he had a beautiful smile.

I wish I could say those are the qualities I noticed first, but it is hard to see those things when there is a massive cock inches from your face. It was so huge it totally blocked out the pool in the background. He was like porno huge. I don't know if it was from shock or wishful thinking but I just laid there staring with my mouth wide open.

He bent down and stuck out his hand, "My name is Uwa." Of course I just laid there like a fucking zombie. So he continued. "What might your name be?"

"Sara. Sara McNeil. There is no 'h' in Sara." How fucking retarded. Who says their entire name and then says no 'h'?

"Hello Sara McNeil, no 'h'. I saw that your friends abandoned you and left you all alone. So I thought I would come over and introduce myself." He pointed to the seat next to me. "Do you mind if I join you."

"Sure not at all," I sat up and he help adjust my seat before he sat down. I noticed he had a thick industrial steel collar locked around his neck. "I don't recall seeing you earlier."

"I just arrived a little after lunch. It is such a lovely day I decided to join everyone out here by the pool."

"How long have you been a submissive?"

"In my professional life I'm a senior partner at a law firm. In my real life I feel that I have always been a submissive. I have just found the courage to explore this side of me a couple of years ago. What about you? How long have you been into the life style?"

"I met my Mistress a little over a year ago. I guess you can say she introduced me to the life style, but it's more like she awoken that part of me. I've never heard of a submissive until after I met her." Maybe it was the sound of his voice that put me at ease, or maybe I'm just a slut. I turned and sat on the side of my seat facing Uwa. I spread my legs about shoulder length apart. I could feel the cool

54

breeze against my moist pussy. "Now it seems as if this is who I always was and everything else was a lie."

"I know what you mean." His voice was as rich and silky as his skin. "Do you work or go to university?"

"I'm in college. I'm sort of undeclared at the moment. I'm leaning towards business or psychology."

"If you had to declare a major today which would you choose?"

"Psychology, but if I go that route I would want to become a medical doctor."

I swear Justine must have built in radar for black men. She and Elyse came slinking up, soak and wet, dripping water everywhere. Justine sat beside me and Elyse stood behind me and started messaging my shoulders.

Elyse asked, "Who's your friend Babe Gurl?"

I rolled my eyes. Uwa smiled and looked into my eyes, "Babe Gurl. I like that. It fits you. You have a very soft face." He stood up and held out his hand to Elyse. "My Name is Uwa."

Elyse shook his hand and responded, "I'm Elyse." She paused for Justine to respond as Uwa stood up and held out his hand towards her. Justine must have been dumb struck after coming face to face with the massive beast between Uwa's legs. She held out her hand but didn't respond. Elyse finished the introductions. "The mute is Justine."

When Uwa shook Justine's hand it seemed to pull her back into reality. Justine smiled and replied. "Sorry, I was distracted."

Uwa smiled and sat down.

Elyse gently guided my head back, kissed me on my forehead and flashed a sheepish smile. "Babe Gurl, we were wondering if you could go get us a couple of towels. We don't want to drip all over the floor."

Justine placed her hand on my leg and started slightly rubbing. "We should have brought them out with us, but we weren't thinking."

Without warning she slipped her two middle fingers between my legs. I was so wet her entire hand would have slipped right in without any resistance. Her thumb pressed firmly against my clit. I had to bite my lower lip to stop from moaning, as she pressed down with circular motions.

She pulled her fingers out and held them up to my face. She licked her lips as she taunted me. "Did we interrupt anything?"

I opened my mouth to protest. Before I could make a sound she shoved her fingers into my mouth. I instinctively sucked and licked them clean. I was humiliated and excited all at the same time. I couldn't look Uwa in the eye. I know, yes I am a submissive, but do I have to make it so easy?

When Justine removed her fingers from my mouth I quickly got up and walked as quickly as I could towards our room. I didn't even bother to get dressed. I wasn't angry or upset with her. I was upset with myself. I was excited, I enjoyed it all. I enjoyed the attention Uwa was giving me. I enjoyed imagining him ravishing me. I enjoyed the way Elyse and Justine teased, humiliated and used me.

If the three of them were to take me right then and there I would have given myself to them. I would have betrayed myself and my Mistress, for a second time. Or maybe it was what she wanted? Maybe this is all some sick test?

When I returned with the towels Uwa was gone. I scanned the area, but couldn't find him. Of course Justine and Elyse were right where I left them. I handed them each a towel and got dressed.

As Elyse got dressed she broke the silence, "Don't worry Babe Gurl, you will see him again."

I tried to sound as uninterested as possible. "Why would I care to see him again?"

Elyse stuck her hand under my dress. "You're still wet."

Once again I was speechless. Justine saved me, "We should get back to our room and get ready for dinner. While you were gone, they asked us to set the main table tonight."

I stepped back and freed myself from Elyse's probing fingers. "Why tonight? I thought our actual training didn't start until the morning."

Justine tossed her towel to me. "I don't know Babe Gurl. Maybe you should ask Mistress Julie when you see her later tonight."

Elyse tossed her towel to me as well, as we headed back to our room.

Just as we were about to walk into our room Matt walked up. "Come with me ladies. I've been looking all over for you. It's time for your exams."

"We have to prepare for dinner", Justine replied.

"You'll have plenty of time for that. This will not take that long."

We followed Matt back to the medical office. "Get undressed". He ordered. He handed us each a clipboard and pointed to some seats in the waiting area. We got undressed, sat down and filled out the forms. It was the usual boring medical background stuff.

About fifteen minutes later Matt returned and motioned for us to follow him. He weighed us, took our height and measurements. He took our blood pressure as well.

Matt then led us to an exam room with three exam tables, with stirrups. "On the table ladies and put your legs in the stirrups. Doctor Elkins will be in to start your examinations in a few moments."

Before we could ask any questions Matt left the room. No one said a word. We just took our positions on an exam table and waited. I don't know, but there is something a little uneasy about being examined like this with two other girls in the room. We didn't even look at each other.

Doctor Elkins didn't speak. He got right down to business. He gave each of us a thorough exam. Matt of course was right there taking notes. For me gyno exams always feel like an invasion of my person. Having Justine and Elyse there made it worse. I'm sure they felt the same.

When the exam was over Matt brought our cloths in, we got dressed. I don't remember any of us saying a word during the examination or on our way back to our room. Just thinking about it is sort of humiliating.

Dinner is Server

When we returned to our room there were three black silk French maid uniforms laid out on each of our beds. The uniforms had white ruffles around the hems of the dress. The back had white lace. The apron was sort of a full apron that had lacey shoulder straps, but it didn't cover the top of the uniform. It just sort of covered the middle of the bottom of the dress and it wrapped around and tied off in the back. We had half inch pumps, thank goodness, and real silk mid-thigh white stockings with a black bow on each one, complete with black and white lacey garter belts. We also had black and white lacey chokers and black and white lacey hair bands. The length of the dress came down just below our crotch area, just low enough to expose our black lacey French cut panties with the cut away crotch. Every time we bend over or stoop down the panties part exposing us for everyone to see.

I wish they had given us bras. Justine laced up my dress so tight it was hard to breathe and my nipples were showing through my top. Elyse said it wasn't that noticeable, because my breast wasn't all that big anyway. I admit no one has ever come up to me and said look at the pair on that hottie. My nipples have a way of making themselves known.

Justine looked at the clock, "We should get going. We have to be in the main dining hall in five minutes."

Elyse commented as we walked out the door. "It looks like the honeymoon is over. Now we have to earn our keep."

When we entered the dining hall we saw what looked like all of the other submissive gathered around one of the dungeon masters, who were speaking to them. The girls were dressed similar to us, except their uniforms weren't as fancy. The men wore only leather G-strings and a black bowtie.

We started walking towards the others and then I heard Uwa, "Babe Gurl!"

I turned towards the sound of his voice. He was standing next to the head table with two other men. They were wearing almost the same uniform the other men wore, except they wore silk white cuffs and collars. He waved us over. I don't know why but I was excited to see him. I could feel my heart flutter and it seemed as if someone turned the heat up in the room. By the time I walked over to him my palms were all sweaty.

He gave the three of us hugs. "Mistress Julie will be with us shortly."

I figured now was as good as time as any to ask, "Is Mistress Julie your Mistress?"

"No, I belong to Mistress Kelly."

"Why are we up here? And why are we dressed differently?"

Uwa looked surprised that I asked that question. "Our Mistresses run or will run this estate."

Justine asked, "There aren't any men?"

Uwa answered, "This estate is divided into two sections the dungeon which we are at now and the private club. Our six Mistresses will run this estate. There is another estate on the east coast which is identical to this one, except it is sun by six Masters. Master Adams and Mistress Julie own estates worldwide. Some are run by both Masters and Mistresses. No two estates are the same."

Before we could ask any more questions Mistress Julie walked up behind us. "As usual Uwa you are very well informed. However the question and answer session will have to wait. Tonight you will be serving your Mistresses. Elyse your Mistress will not be here until the morning. Tonight you will serve me."

"Yes Mistress," Elyse replied with her eyes slightly lowered. I could hear the disappointment in her voice.

Mistress Julie continued. "Before each meal you will set the table for your respective Mistress. The waiters will serve the meals, but you will clear the settings after each course and keep your Mistress glasses filled. You will also attend to any other needs your

60

Mistresses have. Next to your perches you will notice the tables to your right. That is where you will place the china and silverware you remove from your Mistresses setting. After each meal you will clear the tables."

Mistress Julie points to Elyse. "You will wear these uniforms at all times, unless instructed otherwise. When you return to your rooms you will find your closets stocked with enough uniforms to get you through at least a week and a half. Other gear will be added as needed. Your dirty clothes and uniforms will be collected each day and returned once they are cleaned."

Mistress Julie points to the perches. "Once you initially set the table you will lock the collar chained to your perch around your neck. At the end of the meal or if your Mistress gives you leave your Mistress will unlock the collars. When you are not tending your Mistress or being fed by your Mistress you are to kneel on your perch with your backs straight and heads forward, unless instructed otherwise. Are there any questions?"

We all answered, "No Mistress."

Mistress Julie turned to leave, but turned back, "One last thing. I know everyone will be excited to see your Mistress. There will be no public displays of affection. You will be given private time with your Mistress later this evening and afterwards several times throughout the day. That is your private time with your Mistress. All other times you are in training. Your Mistress may utilize your private time as she sees fit. It may be used for punishment, your Mistress pleasure, your pleasure or free time."

Mistress Julie walks away. We start setting our Mistress place. No one spoke. We just went about our duties. One by one we chained ourselves to our respective perches and awaited our Mistress.

The Masters and Mistresses enter the dining hall un-ceremonial. They scan the room searching for their submissive. Some take their seat without acknowledging their submissive. Others give a short greeting and even exchange a few words.

Elyse's perch was empty along with her Mistress' place. Instead Elyse was chained to the perch reserved for Mistress Julie's submissive, which was just to the right of me. I noticed Elyse seemed a bit sad as the other Mistresses and Masters were being reunited with their submissive. So I leaned over and asked, "Are you going to be alright."

She looked over at me and paused a few seconds. "I'll be alright. Mistress will be here in the morning and we'll be together soon. Besides I'm sure Mistress Julie will keep me busy enough."

"Is your Mistress coming in from England?" I can't help it, I'm a busy body. These types of questions just leap out of my mouth.

"No she's been with Mater Adams and Mistress Julie for the past month."

"You mean she's here? If she's here why can't she join us?"

A somber look came over her face. "You know Babe Gurl; sometimes you ask too many questions."

"I'm sorry I didn't mean to get so personal."

"Yes you did, but that's alright. I still love you." She smiles and continues. "I don't know the details but she had been talking with them for a while and then they recalled her to the dungeon. I hadn't heard from or seen her until I received a notice a few days ago. I was ordered to join her at the dungeon. I was told that my lease and belongings would be taken care of. The other night they came to my apartment and took me."

I wanted to ask more but Elyse turned and face forward. So I took it as a sign to back off. Whatever is going on is none of my business. So I will have to wait until later to get more information.

Uwa is about six foot four inches tall. His Mistress is gorgeous. She's very slender, but not anorexic about six feet two. Her high heels bring her to just about his height. Her eyes are grey and her hair is snow white. Her skin is milk white. She has a strong southern belle accent. It sounds like she's from Georgia or maybe

Alabama. I'm bad at accents. She has flawless legs that go on forever. Together their contrast is so extreme they actually work.

She barely acknowledges him as she walks in. None the less there was a connection between them. I can't explain it, but you could feel it in the air. Before she turns the corner of the main table, Uwa has her chair pulled out awaiting her. After she adjusts her seat he pours her a glass of water, which she immediately reaches for. It is as if he anticipates her every movement before she makes it. She waves him off and he returns to his perch.

Mistress Julie, Mistress Kimberly and my Mistress entered the dining hall. I know it only been a day, but it was as if I had been away for a month. I was so excited my heart was pounding. I wanted to leap off the perch and smother her with kisses. But I managed to control myself. I followed Uwa's example and had Mistress's Chair pulled out for her. Justine and Elyse did the same. We also filled their glasses and then returned to our perches.

About halfway through the main course Mistress motioned for me, "Mi amor." I walked over to her and she pointed to the floor next to her, "Siéntese."

I sat down on the floor next to her. You know it's funny. I can't speak a word of Spanish to save my life. Yet I can understand more and more Spanish each day. She handed me her plate. She had portioned off some food and set it to the side for me. She hadn't eaten off it or anything. It wouldn't have mattered to me if she had. I have eaten behind her before. I saw that they were beginning to serve desert so I ate quickly so I could clear Mistress' place before her desert was served. For desert we had strawberries and cream. She hand fed me as I sat by her side.

After desert we sat on our perches while our Mistresses drank coffee and talked, after about thirty minutes or so Masters and Mistresses started leading their submissive away. Justine waved slightly to me as she followed Mistress Kimberly.

Mistress Julie unchained Elyse and instructed her, "Return to your room." Elyse nodded and walked away. She didn't look at me or anyone else for that matter. It must have been hard for her to be the only one without her Mistress present. I wish there was something I could do to comfort her.

Mistress Yvonne unchained me, "Come with me."

I followed her. I don't know why, but as we passed Uwa and his Mistress, I wiggled my ass at him slightly when no one was looking. I swear that man has the quickest hands in the world. He gave my ass a light pinch. It wasn't hard and didn't leave a mark. I looked back to see him mouth the words, *'Watch it Babe Gurl'*. I don't know why I did that, but it was fun and made me feel naughty.

Those of us who were at the main table, with the exception of Elyse, were lead out of the dungeon and to the main Mansion. We were lead to separate sections of the Mansion. The Mansion is four stories high. We walked up to the fourth floor. Mistress Kimberly and Justine went to the third floor. Floors two through four each had two doors at either end of the hallways. Mistress Kimberly led Justine to the room to the right. We also went to the room to the right on our floor.

When Mistress opened the door it was as if we stepped into a Penthouse. Mistress closed the door and smiled, "Go ahead look around. It's ours."

"What do you mean, it's ours?"

"This is where we live. During your training you will stay at the dungeon. Of course we will spend some private time here together."

"What about school?"

"We are not that far. Once school starts we can drive there in about forty five minutes, or there is a driver who will drive us there and pick us up."

"What about jobs? How can we afford to live here?"

"We don't have to pay to stay here. It comes with our new jobs here at the dungeon, if you want it?"

"I don't understand." I was more than a bit confused.

"I'll explain later. Come, let me show you around." Mistress Yvonne waved her arms to showcase the room we were standing in. "This is the foyer. This is where we can entertain like one or two people without them coming all of the way in. It also has a walk in coat closet. There is also a washroom with a toilet."

I thought we were standing in the living room. To the left of the room there was an old Victorian style sofa and two matching love seats caddie cornered, one on each side, with a marble coffee table in the center. The coat closet, more like a small room, was to the right and next to it on the west wall was the washroom. Directly across from the main entrance were double wooden handcrafted wooden doors, which led to the main penthouse.

The double doors glided open with ease. And they closed automatically behind you. Now Mistress Yvonne calls this the sitting room. I have always called it a living room. Anyways it was huge. The entire penthouse was fully decorated in old Victorian antique furniture. Back and to the left is the formal dining area. To the left of that was a smaller breakfast nook and the kitchen. I turned to Mistress, "I thought the kitchen would be larger."

"Normally we will take all of our meals with the others in the main dining room downstairs. This is when we decide to cook ourselves or entertain private guest."

"So we have servants?

"No, the Mansion has employees to tend to our overall needs. I have you to tend to my needs." Mistress licked her lips and flashed a seductive smile.

I could live with that. I couldn't help but smile with excitement, "Yes Mistress."

To the left of the sitting room and just south of the main formal dining area is a Louis XV 18th Century Steinway Grand Piano. There were antique tables and chairs around the piano, I guess so that people can sit and listen to whoever is playing. Behind that is a hand carved wooden door which leads to a walk in pantry.

Behind the sitting area was an entertainment area with a huge ass plasma television with surround sound. There is a bunch of other gizmos that neither of us knows anything about. I'm just thankful the clock on the Blu-ray DVD player was set.

On the right wall is another set of double hand carved wooden doors. Whoever designed this penthouse sure liked wood. Any way the doors led to the Master Bedroom. The 18th century theme was prevalent throughout the bedroom as well. There was a huge ass Victorian style bed with a canopy and veil. Four to five people could easily fit on it. On the back wall was a sliding glass door which led to a balcony with a Jacuzzi, tables with umbrellas, those torch lamps and patio chairs. The balcony ran the length of our penthouse suite. In the far corner there is a white picket fence with a lawn and a doghouse with the word '*Bitch*' carved over the doorway.

I point to the doghouse, "Is that where I sleep?"

"Only when you piss me off," I was expecting a smile, but Mistress just continued with the tour.

To the right there is a wash area, where you can brush your teeth and wash your hands. There are four sinks, each with its own mirrored medicine cabinets. To the left of that is the toilet room. It is considerably large considering there is only a toilet and one of those bidet toilets; you know the ones that squirt water up your ass.

Against the back wall was a walk in closet with one of those carousels that moved your closes around so you don't have to go searching for closes. There is a dressing area, complete with one of those boxes you stand on when the tailor is fitting your clothes and a double vanity station in the dressing room.

There is a door in the closet that leads to the bathroom. In the bathroom is a large standalone porcelain tub, with solid brass legs and pluming. There is a waterfall shower that comes out of the wall. There is no shower curtain. There is a drain in the middle of the floor so I guess it doesn't matter if the floor gets wet.

Mistress starts running bath water. She instructs me, "Get undressed."

I eagerly undressed as Mistress undressed as well. She added bath oil to the water and tested it for temperature. She turned off the water and got into the tub. She slid back to the far end of the tub opposite the faucets. I knelt down next to the tub. I pulled her hair forward and started washing her back with one of those organic sponges.

After about two minutes Mistress looked up and pulled me to her. She gave me a deep, passionate kiss. Her warm tongue invaded my willing mouth. "Get in," she ordered.

"Yes Mistress," I got in and sat facing her."

"No, turn around and lean back against me."

"Yes Mistress."

Before I could get fully seated Mistress pulled me as close to her as possible, her breast where firmly against my back. She reached around me with both hands and grabbed by breast. Holding me securely in place we continue kissing. She squeezes and pulls my nipples as hard as she could. It hurt like hell, but I didn't dare try to stop her.

I began to squirm. She wrapped her legs around my body and used them to spread my legs apart and lock me into place. All I could do was to endure. Not that I'm complaining, the pain was very erotic. Mistress slid her right hand down my stomach and between my legs. She began to masturbate me. I was no match for the power in her legs. She pulled back my hood and exposed my clit. She pinched my clit. It sent a shockwave of pain and pleasure racing through my entire body. I had an instant orgasm.

I don't know why I did what I did next. Everything was going so well. I was relaxing in Mistress' arms. She kissed me and I bit her lower lip. I didn't bite her hard. It was more of a love bite. I didn't even leave a mark.

"You fucking bratty bitch." She grabbed me by my hair and forced me over the side of the tub. She got out and started spanking my soaking wet ass with her hand. She wasn't mad or anything. But my wet ass amplified each smack as it echoed off the walls. A few well-placed smacks on my legs signaled me to spread my legs. Leaving me fully exposed. She didn't stop until my ass was bright red and on fire. I didn't cry out once. I was so proud of myself.

Mistress pulled me up by my hair. It felt good to have my ass sitting in the water again. She put her left leg up on the tub and forced my face between her legs.

I love the taste of my Mistress' pussy. But I was feeling especially bratty tonight. So I boxed my lips and refused to lick her. Suddenly I felt a sting across my back I wasn't expecting. I figured I would earn another spanking and eventually I would make it up to Mistress by being extra attentive to her. But where in the fuck did she get that fucking two-throng leather strap from. I didn't see her bring it in with her.

She ripped into my back and exposed ass. She strapped my legs and I did my best to keep my legs open, but each time she hit my pussy or asshole I screamed in pain and pulled my legs closed. But I quickly spread my legs again when she strapped my legs. I did my best to lick Mistress' pussy, but it was hard to concentrate. After about fifty or so strokes my entire body was quivering and my face was stained with tears.

When Mistress finally put that fucking strap down, I buried my face between her thighs. I shoved my tongue as deep inside of her pussy as I could. I sucked her cunt so hard she had multiple orgasms. I licked up every drop. She wasn't angry or anything, but

I didn't want to push it tonight. I really missed her and I wanted things to be perfect for her tonight.

Mistress pulls the drain on the tub, "Get out."

I got out and removed a towel from the towel rack. I started drying Mistress off.

As I finished drying my breasts Mistress gave my nipples one last twist and said, "Dry off and crawl your bratty ass out to our room." She turned and left.

After I dried off I crawled into our room as instructed. Mistress was in bed. She pulled back the sheets to reveal that she was naked. "Get up, turn out the lights and get your ass over here," she instructed.

"Yes Mistress." I turned out the lights. It took a while for my eyes to adjust to the dark, but I made my way to the bed and crawled under the sheets. It felt good to be in her arms again.

Mistress whispered in my ear, "Tonight I'm Yvonne and you are Sara. I'm not your Mistress and you are not my submissive. I am just a girl in love with you."

"You have never stopped being Yvonne to me. But now you are more. You are my Mistress and I am your slave. I am also a girl very much in love with you as well."

"It's still not too late to change your mind."

"Yes it is. This is who you are. This is who we are. I … we can't go back now. We can only go forward, together."

Mistress' face was coming into focus and I could see the tears streaming down her face. I don't know why she is so afraid of losing me. I can't imagine anything that could break us apart. We fell asleep in each other's arms as we had so many times before. It felt like home again.

Ghosts of the Past

Mistress woke me up around five the next morning by tossing a jogging outfit next to me. "Get up and get dressed, stretch and meet me in the sitting room in twenty minutes."

"Yes Mistress." I got up, washed up and got dressed. I'm not much on stretching. Mistress has tried to teach me how to warm up, but exercise has never been my thing. I do aerobics and things like that, but not all out running and working out on the machines. I do the best I can when she gets on her exercise kick.

I met Mistress outside and we went downstairs and out back. Mistress took me by my arm. "Every morning at five thirty sharp you are to meet me out here, rain or shine, unless instructed otherwise. We will go for a brief jog around the estate and then head to the gym for a workout."

"Yes Mistress." She knows I hate that jock work out she does.

"I know you didn't do a proper warm up. You never do. I am going to show you one last time. After today if you don't get it right, I will strip you naked spank you on the spot and you will complete your workout completely nude. Is that clear?"

"Yes Mistress."

"After our morning workout you will return to your dorm room, shower and get dress for the rest of the day."

We had a light workout this morning. We were done by six twenty. Justine was at the gym as well working out with Mistress Kimberly. Not that I don't enjoy my time with Mistress, but if I have to lift one more free weight my arms are going to fall off. So I had another brilliant idea, "Mistress. It looks as if Mistress Kimberly and Justine workout about the same time we do. Would it be possible for us to work out together?"

"Not a bad idea. Stay here while I speak with Mistress Kimberly." Mistress walked over to Mistress Kimberly. They spoke for a while and then Mistress motioned for me.

I walked over to where they were standing. "Yes Mistress."

Mistress Kimberly stated, "Justine, Elyse and you will meet us every morning for our workout."

"Yes Ma'am," I responded. I then asked Mistress Yvonne, "Since I am not good with the free weights can Elyse and I work out with Justine after our run?" Justine does that ballerina stretching crap, but it's a lot better than that jock power workout Mistress does. Besides I'm really too much of a distraction. I do all of the exercises wrong. According to Mistress I work out like a girl. I just don't see the point. Besides I like being a girl.

Mistress Yvonne looked over at Justine working out. "Sure, why not. But if I catch the three of you fucking around there will be hell to pay." She doesn't think Justine does a "*REAL*" work out, but I don't think she wants my drama. She takes her work outs serious.

"Thank you Mistress."

Mistress Yvonne pointed towards the dungeon. "The two of you need to head back to your dorm and get ready for breakfast."

I reminded Mistress, "We need to go back and get our uniforms."

"Your wardrobes should be fully stocked and you should have fresh uniforms."

"Yes Mistress." I got Justine and we walked back to the dorms. I was so excited, especially for Elyse. She gets to be with her Mistress today. I hope they give her time with her Mistress tonight. It looks as if it was going to be a beautiful day, not too hot and not too cold.

When we got back to our room the lights were out, so Justine turned them on. We noticed that none of the beds have been slept in. Our uniforms were laid out on our beds. Justine called out, "Elyse are you here?" There was no answer.

I replied, "Maybe she went to the dining hall."

"Not without her uniform."

71

"Maybe she's working out."

"Maybe," Justine started to undress. We had better take a quick shower and get dressed."

As we were walking to the shower the door opened and Elyse walked in. She was wearing a Catholic Schoolgirl uniform. Her white blouse was a few sizes too small and really showcased her breast. Her plaid shirt barely covered her ass. She flashed her lacey white panties with every step.

"Where in the hell have you been?" Justine blurted out as if she was the boss of us. She can be a bossy little bitch for a submissive.

Elyse entire face lit up. "Master Adams released me to my Mistress after diner. I spent the night with her." Elyse started undressing.

"So we finally get to meet your Mistress." I asked, "What is her name?"

Before Elyse could respond Justine interrupted. "We don't have time for small talk. We can do updates later. We have less than fifteen minutes to get showered, dressed and to the dining hall."

"Who died and made you head bitch?" I really should learn to not say the first thing that pops into my head.

Elyse walked up behind me and grabbed my breasts from behind. She held me secure and started twisting my nipples. I was about to let out a scream, but Justine was so close our lips were touching. Suddenly I knew my place. I wasn't scared, but I felt powerless.

Justine reached back and spread my ass as wide apart as she could. She spoke in a very authoritative whisper. "Listen Babe Gurl, you know I love you. You will always be my main bitch. But you have to learn your place. I know your Mistress is top pussy around here. But in this room your ass serves us. As for whom the fuck is in charge that is for the grownups to work out. Now get your ass in the shower."

When they released me, I didn't say a word. I ran straight to the shower. I wasn't scared and I wasn't hurt, but I didn't want them to see me cry. It's hard to explain. Things were rapidly becoming more and more complex and at times felt out of control. At that moment I really felt as if I belonged. I know it sounds wired, but that's how I felt. I really don't know why in the hell I was crying.

I turned on all three shower heads. I stood under the one of them and let the tears flow. I wasn't weeping or crying out loud. I made no sound; with the water running no one could tell I was having a cry. I wasn't sad. I wasn't mad. I wasn't scared and I wasn't hurt. I don't know how to explain what I was feeling at that moment, because I don't understand it myself. But the closest I can explain it is that I felt a release. It felt right. This crazy world I fell into made since for that one brief moment.

There was an excitement in the air during setup for breakfast. Everyone was anticipating what the day would bring. I spent most of the morning flirting with Uwa. He seemed extremely happy and touchy today. I admit I don't know him all that well, but it seemed a bit out of character for him. I just went with it, besides it made the time pass.

After we chained ourselves to our perches, time seemed to stand still. Finally the Masters and Mistresses entered the dining hall. Only this time it was very ordered. They were all dressed completely in black. After they have all been seated one by one the Mistresses who sit at the main table entered the room.

I heard Elyse chains clink as she sat up a little taller. I glanced over at her and I saw her face light up. She was almost giddy.

Then I heard Justine exclaim under her breath, "holy fuck!" Her expression was one of total shock.

At that moment Elyse's Mistress passed by my perch. "What the Fuck!" The hall was quite so my outburst was amplified even more. A deep stillness enveloped the dining hall. It was as if all of the life was drained out of my body. "What the fuck are you doing here bitch!"

A sharp slap across my face from my Mistress quickly followed. "Sara!"

I stood up and pointed at Elyse's Mistress, "That fucking cunt …"

Mistress stopped me in mid-sentence three sharp slaps across my face each one harder than the last.

Mistress Yvonne ordered me in Spanish, "Siéntate y cállate! No quiero escuchar otro sonido de usted!"

I knew better to say another word, despite the circumstances. When Mistress scolds me entirely in Spanish she means business. I retreated to my perch, with tears of anger streaming down my face. I looked over at Elyse. She was in total shock mixed with anger. I wanted to tell her about her so called Mistress. I wanted to tell everyone what she did to me. I don't care how they dress her up or what they call her, that fucking bitch, Robyn, is no Mistress.

I was so angry I could spit fire. I don't know how, but I completed service to my Mistress, although it wasn't easy. I did my best not to look in Robyn's direction.

After breakfast Mistress Yvonne ordered, "The three of you stay here. We need to set some ground rules." I started to object, but Mistress looked me and in the most commanding voice I ever heard from her ordered, "Cállate!" I'm guessing that means *'shut the fuck up'*. Why she was angry at me, I don't know. But I sat there statutes awaiting her next command.

After everyone left the dining hall, our Mistresses walked around to the front of the table. Only the staff remained and went about their duties as if we weren't there.

Mistress Yvonne addressed Elyse first, "Elyse I know you are confused and maybe a bit angry. I will do my best to explain what is going on. If you need any further explanation I suggest you take it up with your Mistress later during your free time."

Elyse looked at Robyn and then back at Mistress Yvonne and replied, "Yes ma'am."

Mistress Yvonne continued, "Until I spoke with Mistress Julie a couple days ago I had no idea Mistress Robyn would be joining us.

Master Adams and Mistress Julie are aware of what happened between Mistress Robyn and Sara."

I couldn't contain myself, "They know she attacked me?"

Mistress Yvonne took a step forward and looked me directly in the eyes. "Yes, they know. They also know what we did to her. It's complicated, but Mistress Robyn has earned the right to take her place not only at this table but at the Mansion."

Justine was just as angry as I was. She interjected, "And just how did she manage that?"

Mistress Kimberly snapped at her, "That is none of your business! You are not to concern yourself with the affairs of Master Adams and Mistress Julie."

I snapped back, "Maybe I should ask Master Adams myself?"

Mistress Yvonne pounded her fist down on the table. "You will do no such a thing. Their judgment is final and you will not question it any further."

The sound of Robyn's voice sent a chill down my spine. I could hear a slight tremble in her voice as she spoke. "I can't take back what happened and I can't undo the past. I do regret my actions and the hurt I caused you. I accept that we will never be friends, but we have to find a way to coexist."

Mistress Yvonne continued, "I love you Sara. And I hate that I had to keep this from you. My stomach has been in knots for the past three days. But this is our home. But it is also Mistress Robyn's and Elyse home as well."

I tried to fight back the tears, but it was like trying to stop a flood. I felt helpless as I looked at my Mistress, my lover and replied, "I don't know what to do. I love you too, but I don't know if I can do this. It is all happening too fast."

Mistress Yvonne continued, "I'm going to excuse the three of you from today's training. It is only an orientation. Unfortunately the three of us must attend. If you decide to stay Sara, we are all going to have to find a way to work and live together. I will have to have your answer after dinner tonight." All three Mistresses turned and walked away. Mistress Yvonne stopped just before she walked out the door and added, "Mi amor. I will not blame you if you decide to leave the Estate. But if you do, we will leave together."

You could have heard a pin drop at that moment. I watched as my Mistress walked away without me. After a few minutes we unchained ourselves and walked back to our room.

When we walked into our room, I was surprised to find Robyn there. Elyse ran over and knelt at Robyn's feet in complete submission.

Robyn guided her to her feet and walked her over to her bed and they sat down. Justine sat next to me on my bed. Robyn began to speak. "I met Yvonne during her first year in college. She was dating Kimberly. Shortly after they broke up Yvonne and I started dating. I introduced Yvonne and Kimberly to Mistress Julie. She agreed to train the three of us, at first as her slaves, but later she saw we were all dominate so she got permission from Master Adams to mentor us as Mistresses to run this Estate. For short while we were sister slaves, I became the dominate one. It sort of carried over when we started our mentorship as Mistresses. The problem is that I fell in love and all I wanted to do was serve Yvonne. So I gave up my position to become Yvonne's slave. Only it didn't work out between us and we broke up."

Elyse asked, "So you continued your mentorship as a Mistress?"

Robyn continued, "No. Master Adams refused to accept me back as a Mistress. He prohibited Mistress Julie from even taking me back as her slave. So I was out. Unless I could find another Mistress to take me in I would not be allowed back at the Mansion." She looked and directly at me, "And then I saw you. It's not that I wanted Yvonne back, it's just that you now had the position I walked away from. What I did to you was wrong and I apologize. Yvonne loves you and if you leave she will follow. Once she does that she cannot come back. Don't throw this away because of what I did."

Justine asked, "Master Adams took you back, why?"

Robyn takes hold of Elyse's hand. "After what happened between us I decided to walk away from this life style. That didn't last long. I met Elyse at an adult fetish shop I worked at and we started dating. I went to Master Adam and begged him for a second chance. I was severely punished for what I did to you and I had to serve him for six months before he agreed to allow Mistress Julie to mentor me again. He just gave the ok a week ago. I sent for Elyse and here we are." Robyn got up and walked towards the door. She stopped at the door, looked and back and asked me, "Didn't you use to be a blonde?"

Of course I answered like a trained seal. "I was sort of a dirty blonde. I dyed it back to my natural color, boring ass brown."

"For what it's worth your natural color suits you." She walked out, closing the door behind her.

We sat there for about five minutes without saying a word. There were latex miniskirts and bras on our beds along with three inch patent leather pumps. I got up and walked over to Elyse and handed her the outfit on her bed. "The two of you should get dressed and go join your Mistresses. I need to be alone."

Elyse looked down and said, "I still don't know exactly what happened, but I'm sorry. I didn't know."

"You have nothing to be sorry about," I answered. "You did nothing to me."

Justine asked, "Are you alright? Do you want to talk?"

"I will be fine," I answered. "We will talk after lunch."

I got into bed and pulled the covers over my head. I didn't want them to see me cry. It's not like Justine hasn't seen me cry before.

But somehow this was different. I wasn't ready to share my emotions. I just wanted to feel them.

I was torn. Part of me wanted to run away and hide. Part of me wanted to scream, shout and throw a fit. Part of me wanted to fight. And part of me just wanted to be held. I just don't know which part to give into first, so I cried.

Putting the Past behind Us

If there is one thing I know how to do is to make an entrance. I don't know what they were talking about, but there was a dead silence when I walked into the dungeon bare ass naked. I stood at the doorway until Mistress Yvonne motioned for me to come to her. I walked over and knelt at my Mistress feet and sat up straight with my hands behind my back.

Mistress Yvonne asked, "Are you sure?"

"Yes Mistress," I answered.

Mistress pointed to a table against the wall. "Go get the Rosewood paddle, the one with the holes."

"Yes Mistress," I walked over to the table and picked up the paddle as instructed. I took it back to my Mistress.

I knelt down and hand it to my Mistress. She took the paddle from me. "Open your mouth."

I did as instructed. She placed the handle of the paddle in my mouth. I was careful to not get teeth marks on the paddle while I held it firmly in my mouth.

Mistress Yvonne grabbed a handful of my hair and turned my head to face Robyn. "Before I can allow you to serve me, you have to be properly punished for the disrespect you showed Mistress Robyn this morning."

"Yes Mistress," I crawled over to Robyn and handed her the paddle. As she leaned forward to take the paddle I whispered in her ear, "Do you love Elyse?"

"Yes," she answered.

"I don't forgive you. I love my Mistress and I do this for her."

Robyn whispered as she pulled me over her lap, "Your Mistress is very lucky."

Before I was completely across her lap she laid into my ass. I could hear the paddle whistling through the air as it raced towards my unprotected ass. All I could do was dig in. In seconds my ass was on fire. I refused to cry or scream out in pain. I was doing just fine until she started pulling my cheeks apart and talking.

"For as long as you are here, you will respect every Mistress and Master here, is that clear?" Robyn spoke in rhythm with each stroke.

"Yes ma'am, yes Mistress." I yelped fighting back the tears as my voice cracked. It wasn't a long spanking. But it was a hard and steady spanking. I was crying like a baby when she let me up. I slowly crawled over to my Mistress. I didn't find the comfort I expected. She didn't acknowledge me. That hurt worse than the paddling.

Mistress Yvonne spoke to the room, "We are going to break for lunch. Everyone except Sara is excused. After lunch we will meet back here where you will officially be welcomed by Master Adam and Mistress Julie."

As they left the room, I searched for Uwa. He somehow manages to walkup behind me without anyone, including me, noticing. His deep and heavily accented voice was a comfort to me. "Hang in there Babe Gurl."

I didn't look back to see him. His voice was enough to reassure me. I was afraid he would judge me. I don't know why that was important to me, but it was.

Mistress Yvonne watched Uwa as he walked out the door and turned down the hallway, led by his Mistress. She looked down at me and asked, "Who is he?"

I looked up at her and replied, "Who is who, Mistress?" I knew exactly who she was talking about. I don't know why I said that.

Mistress grabbed me by my hair and lifted me to my feet. "No enrede con mí! The big black man who just called you Babe Gurl, who the hell is he?" She gave my right ear a twist.

I was caught off guard by the sharp slap across my face, delivered by Mistress. I forgot how jealous she can get. "What the fuck? He is no one. His name is Uwa. His Mistress is Mistress Kelly."

Mistress twisted my ear even harder, which caused her to pull my hair at the same time. "Mind your tone with me. I know who Mistress Kelly is and I know who Uwa is. What I'm asking is who the fuck is he to you and why did he call you Babe Gurl?"

"Justine and Elyse started calling me that. I guess it is catching on. I only met Uwa yesterday at the pool. He's just a friend. Since I'm going to be here all summer, I should make friends."

There are those times when you know you should just let it go. And this is definitely one of those times. But I ask you, where is the fun in that? I could see her Latina blood boiling. The trick is to get Mistress to the point where she is speaking Spanglish, a mixture of Spanish and English. Mistress becomes very creative at that point. But if I take it too far, she starts speaking only Spanish, she will just shut down and that's no fun. "Mistress Kelly is hot. Have you known her long?" Yes, I went there.

"Excuse me," Mistress' voice cracked just a little. I caught her totally off guard with that one.

In my most innocent voice I respond, "Nothing. I was just thinking out loud. But you have to admit she does have a nice ass."

Mistress yanked my head back by my hair, "¡Párese su fucking asno arriba bitch! I've got something for your ass." She dragged me out the door, down the hall and into the dining hall.

Mistress didn't say a word to me. I hate it when she doesn't talk. It's hard for me to tell how pissed off she is when she doesn't talk. When we arrived at the dining hall, Mistress gave my sore ass a solid smack and she pointed towards my perch. I was hoping Mistress would have allowed me to dress before lunch. I guess I should have thought about that before I decided to piss her off.

As I made my way to my perch, Mistress went to the kitchen. I just hope she doesn't come back with a fucking bread board or something. My ass can only take so much more. A few minutes later Mistress returned. She didn't bring anything back with her. I was on edge all of lunch. I knew Mistress was up to something, I just didn't know what.

After lunch a waiter brings over one of those sliver trays with a silver cover on it to Mistress. He sets the tray on the table in front of Mistress. He removed the cover and walked back to the kitchen. Fuck me, it was a ginger root. The large end was peeled and craved into the shape of a butt plug.

Mistress pointed towards my perch and motioned for me to stand on it and turn around facing the pole. Mistress tapped her water glass lightly with her fork. "May I have your attention please?" She looked back at me. "Bend forward, spread your legs, and spread your ass."

Mistress stood up and stood behind me. The dining hall was silent as she spoke. "What I'm about to demonstrate is called Figging. It helps your submissive remember his or her place. All you need is a ginger root with one end peeled. Notice that it is carved into the shape of a butt plug." She inserted it into me, while slightly twisting it as she forced it into me. "There is no need for lubrication. The freshly peeled ginger root provides all of the lubrication you will need."

If you have never had a peeled ginger root shoved up your ass before, let me tell you it burns like hell. I had to walk around the remainder of the day with a ginger root up my ass. Eventually the effects wear off, so Mistress was kind enough to replace it frequently with a fresh root.

I sat through the rest of the orientation naked and in total agony. It didn't turn out exactly as I expected. I could barely walk at the end of the day. Mistress was kind enough to allow me to serve her during dinner without the ginger root.

By the next day the swelling went down a bit along with most of the pain. The funny part is that I could still feel the ginger root on and off throughout most of the day. I don't trust nor do I like Mistress Robyn. I guess I have to find a way to tolerate and even obey her. I really don't know if I can do this, but I'm going to try. For one, Mistress seems so happy here. Secondly, I can get used to living in a Mansion.

A Night on the Town

That first week went by fast. I can't believe it was already Friday. We just completed lunch when Mistress Julie approached Uwa and me and handed Uwa the keys to the van. "A friend needs two models for a new line of bondage wear. I'm sending Sara and you to the shoot. The shoot shouldn't take more than a couple of hours. You will however have to stay overnight." Mistress Julie handed Uwa a credit card and cell phone. "Use the card for dinner. I doubt you will make it back in time to eat here. If something comes up give me a call. The address is already programed into the van's GPS. Just look up Master Scott. Go and change into vanilla wear and head out in fifteen minutes."

Before we could respond she walked away barking orders at one of the staff members.

Uwa patted me on my head, "I'll meet you out front in fifteen minutes Babe Gurl."

Vanilla wear … I have everything but Vanilla wear. I went through my closet looking for something that won't stand out like some sicko. I found a Catholic schoolgirl uniform, complete with that little neck tie thingy. The skirt was a bit short, but it would have to do.

I was about to put on a pair of silk panties when Elyse walked in. She took one look at the uniform laid out and reprimanded me. "You don't wear silk panties with a traditional school uniform." She walked over and took them out of my hands. She walked over to the dresser and pulled out a pair of navy blue granny panties. She tossed them to me. "You wear school blue knickers and white knee highs."

If I had a backbone I would have marched right over there and snatch my silk panties right out of her snooty British hands. She can call them school knickers all she wants, but those granny panties went all the way up to my navel.

Of course Elyse marched right over and pulled the waist band down to my hips. "Don't play around." She started dressing me.

After she got my tie on she put my hair up in pigtails. She turned me around and looked me over. She shook her head no, and took out the pigtails and used a scrunch to put my hair back in a ponytail. She turned me around again and nodded, "Perfect."

She kissed me on my lips. Of course I kissed her back. "I have to go", I whispered as I pulled away."

She pulled me back towards her, "Why are you in such a hurry to be Uwa's little schoolgirl slut?'

"I'm not his slut. Mistress Julie is sending us on a photo shoot."

She took me by my ponytail and forced me to my knees. "I know. Mistress Julie sent me in here to get you ready." She pushed me back against the wall. She raised her left leg up against the wall. The slit in her panties parted and exposed her hairless pussy and asshole. She forced my face between her thighs.

I instinctively started licking as I muffled out, "I have to go. Uwa is waiting."

"Then I suggest you work fast." She rubbed her wet pussy in my face.

I didn't put up much of a fight. I didn't have time. So I concentrated on her clitoris. The more I flicked it with my tongue the harder she rode my face. When her clit peeked out from its hood, I was able to run the tip of my tongue just barely between her clit and under her hood. I thought she was going to crush my head with her thighs. I had to pull her towards me to keep her from losing her balance.

"Tell me how you are going to suck his black cock", she taunted me.

I tried to respond and tell her that wasn't going to happen, but it was all I could do to breathe.

She continued, "He is going to face fuck you so hard and deep his cock is going to slam against the back of your throat and work its

85

way down until you choke and loads of thick slobber slips out of your mouth uncontrollably; and when he cum his thick spud will force its way down your throat as you choke and gasp for air."

She pulled my head back a few seconds so I could gasp for air and then forced me back into position. "What a slut, you want him to fuck you. You want him to pin your knees back up to your ears and fuck the shit out of you. You want him to pound his black cock so far up your slutty cunt that you can taste his cum."

Of course none of that was true, or was it? I was wet and on the edge of exploding. My entire body was quivering. Suddenly she thrust against me as her juices flowed. She rubbed her juices all over my face. She pulled me from between her legs by my ponytail and said, "Maybe he just wants to cum in your ass." She pushed me back onto the ground.

I didn't know what to say or do. I just laid there trying to compose myself.

"You better get a move on before he come looking for you." She said with a wicked smile.

I got up and fixed my clothes. I started to walk to the wash room. Elyse grabbed me by my arm and ushered me out the door. "Don't you dare wipe me off your face; I want him to smell me on you."

I was frustrated, humiliated and excited all at the same time. My legs were so weak; I barely made it to the van.

When I got in Uwa asked, "What kept you Babe Gurl? I almost came looking for you."

I just looked out the window and said, "Sorry, I couldn't decide what to wear." Until now I never seriously thought about fucking Uwa, but at that moment I was so horny I would have fucked him right there in the van.

"I like the ponytail", he added as we drove off.

I don't know why, but I flipped him off, without even looking up at him. Of course he just let out this deep rich belly laugh. Even his laugh has an accent to it.

About five minutes into the drive I looked over at him. "I'm sorry. I just hate this outfit."

"You look cute, just like a proper schoolgirl."

I hadn't noticed before, but Uwa was wearing jeans and a tight black tee shirt. "What the fuck? Where did you get those from?"

"The wardrobe", I guess he noticed the dumbass look on my face. He clarified, "The closet."

"I looked. All I could find was this retarded shit."

"Did you rotate the carousal?"

"What the fuck is carousal?"

"Did you notice the three buttons on the wall next to where your clothes are hung?"

"Yeah," I answered timidly.

"Did you ever push any of them?"

"No."

"Well our clothes are on carousal. You press the blue button to rotate to the costumes. Press the red button to rotate to bondage gear. Press the green button to rotate to vanilla wear."

I can't believe none of us ever pressed any of the buttons. I feel so stupid right now. "So all I had to do was push a fucking button to find normal clothes?"

Uwa of course started laughing at me again. "Where did you think all of the outfits were coming from?"

"I really didn't give it a thought."

"What is it like in your world Babe Gurl?"

I'm not sure if that was an insult or not, "Confusing. I look ridiculous."

"You look hot Babe Gurl. Loose the tie and let down a couple of buttons and you will be awesome."

Uwa always seem to say the right things. I forgot about Robyn for the rest of the trip. I just had a normal conversation. I don't remember what exactly we spoke about, but I do know it had nothing to do with the life style. We just spoke as if we were old friends.

I don't know how long we drove, but we finally arrived at an art gallery. I was sort of surprised. I don't know what I expected, but I wasn't expecting an art gallery. Uwa parked in the rear parking lot.

We walked in through the back door. All of the art and fixtures were covered. I was tempted to peak, but Uwa walked so fast and he was headed directly for the offices. I figured I had best keep up.

Uwa knocked on the door and stepped in, "Excuse me. I'm looking for a Master Scott."

I was surprised. Uwa didn't sound very submissive. He was very forceful. I of course stood behind him and didn't utter a word.

This short, sort of portly man emerged, "I'm Master Scott."

Uwa extended his hand. "I'm Uwa." He guided me forward, "This shy creature is Sara McNeil, no 'h'. Mistress Julie informed us you were in need of a couple of models."

Master Scott shook Uwa's hand. "I'm glad you could make it Uwa and Miss. McNeil."

I curtsied, "My pleasure sir." My pleasure sir … who says shit like that? And why the hell did I curtsy? I am such a newb.

Master Scott spoke directly to Uwa, which was perfectly alright with me. "We had a change in plans. We originally were going to do the shoot for our catalog before the exhibit. But we decided to incorporate the shoot into the exhibit. The two of you will actually be part of the exhibit as works of living art." He walked us to the door and pointed to the stair well in the far corner. "Go and find Cheryl. She will take your measurements." Before either of us could respond, he walked away and returned to what he was doing.

"Come Babe Gurl," Uwa the Great commanded as he walked off. Of course I followed. What choice did I have? When we got upstairs it was like a warehouse for perverts. I was like a kid in a candy store. There were two ladies in their forties (I guess) sorting through everything.

Uwa once again took the initiative. "Master Scott sent us up for a Cheryl to take our measurements."

An oriental lady definitely in her mid to late forties emerged from the clutter. "Undress quickly", she ordered.

I removed my panties first and quickly bunched them up and dropped them by my feet. I dropped my blouse on top of them. As soon as we were completely undressed one of the other women gathered up our clothes, folded them and placed them neatly to the side. Cheryl wasn't exactly gentle with her measuring. She was borderline rude. I swear she purposely probed me with her fingers a few times, while taking my measurements. She had us try on several outfits, including a few leather harnesses.

About an hour or so into our fitting, I heard a pleasantly familiar voice. "Master Scott sent us up for a fitting." It was my Mistress, Yvonne and Mistress Kelly was with her.

I was so excited I started towards Mistress. I was quickly stopped by a sharp pinch on my inner thigh by Cheryl.

"Undress and wait", Cheryl barked without even looking up.

She was done with Uwa and me about ten minutes later. As we got dressed Mistress Yvonne and Mistress Kelly took their place in the measuring area. Mistress Yvonne spoke, "The two of you wait for us and we will go get dinner before the exhibit starts."

"Yes Mistress", I replied.

"Yes Mistress Yvonne", Uwa replied in turn.

It didn't take long to measure Mistress Yvonne and Mistress Kelly. They were done in about twenty minutes. We ate a little café about a block away. It was as if we were old friends.

"Mistress …" I started to ask.

89

I was cut off midsentence by Mistress Yvonne. "We are on free time. Call me Yvonne. I'm still your Mistress. I just need to know that I am more than that to you."

I leaned forward and planted a full kiss on Yvonne's lips. I think that was the first real kiss I gave her in a public vanilla setting. "You are everything to me and more."

"I'm sorry about Robyn", Yvonne added abruptly. "I wanted to tell you. I wanted to warn you, but I wasn't allowed."

"It's alright. I think we worked it out." It really wasn't alright. I hated the sight of that bitch, but I didn't want to give this up.

Kelly added, "I'm not a fan of Robyn, but she is going to be living there with us, so we all have to learn to get along."

Dinner was a lot of fun. It has been a long time since I just sat and had fun with Yvonne. She has been so tense lately. There was one thing about dinner that sort of caught me off guard. Uwa's and Kelly's role seemed to have changed. Uwa took charge and he even ordered for her. At one point she even did that lovey dove thing and fed him. It was quite embarrassing to watch.

Being the good friend I am, I had to act quickly and save Uwa from himself. "Since we are being informal and all, exactly what are we being trained for and what will be expected of us?" Both Kelly and Yvonne looked like a couple of deer caught in the headlights. You would have thought I have asked for a definitive answer to the meaning of life as it pertained to the Amazonian Pigmies.

Of course leave it to Uwa to save the day and let them off the hook. "It's getting late. We had best start heading back." He gave me a stern look.

I wasn't really trying to start trouble. I really did want an answer. I just don't get the secrecy. Mistress Yvonne and Mistress Kelly walked ahead as we left the café. I assumed free time was over. Uwa came up behind me as we exited. He slipped his hand under my skirt and patted and then rubbed my bottom over my panties

90

and whispered in my ear, "You ask too many questions Babe Gurl. Sometimes you just have to take things as they come."

I never realized just how large his hands were. They were very strong. He pulled my panties up just before he removed his hand from under my skirt. I reached around to pull them back down. He grabbed my hand and shook his head no. So I was forced to walk the entire way back with my panties up the crack of my ass and pussy. I just hope no one saw him when he did that.

As soon as we walked through the back door of the gallery a man walked up took me by the arm and walked me to a room where he stripped me nude. Another lady pulled me over to a salon chair and pushed me down into it. She spun the chair around and reclined the chair back so my head was over the sink. She started shampooing my hair. While another person. I couldn't see if they were male or female, pulled my legs apart and applied shaving cream to my pussy and started shaving me with a straight razor. I don't know how safe that was, but they seemed to know what they were doing. I felt someone rub my legs checking for stubble I guess. But I shaved this morning so I was alright. The really embarrassing part came when they raised my legs to check my asshole area for hair.

As my hair was drying I received a manicure and pedicure. Then my hair was styled and finally makeup. They applied makeup to my entire body. Afterwards I they put a leather body harness on me. It fit like a glove. There were steel rings all over it. A thick plain black leather collar was placed around my neck along with ankle and wrist restraints.

I was so busy being pampered I didn't hear Mistress Yvonne enter. "Stand up and give me a look", she said.

I stood up and teased her a little by wiggling my butt at her. When I slowly turned around with my hands out, I figured if I played my cards right I can get Mistress all worked up for later tonight. The problem was that when I turned around it was she who took my breath away. I went weak in the knees and had to kneel before I fell over.

Mistress was wearing a black form fitting shinny leather body suit. It was low cut and accented her cleavage perfectly. It didn't have zippers or buttons. It was laced up the front with a single long red leather strap. I guess that is what you call it. She wore matching gloves that came about three quarters of the way up her arms. It was laced with the same red straps as the body suit. Her matching two inch heel boot came about three quarters of the way up her thighs, only the front has a lapel flap that folded down in the front. The boots were laced with the same type of red leather straps. She wore full length red silk stockings with lacy tops. She was carrying a red and black laced riding crop.

Cheryl entered and looked us both over. She pointed at me and told the man who was with her, "Stand her up and get her out of that."

I stood up as he approached. He loosened the body suit I was wearing and I stepped out of it. Not like I was wearing much to begin with, but I felt naked. Cheryl handed Mistress a long red leather leash. "Go claim your bitch and get out there and work the floor" Cheryl told Mistress Yvonne.

Mistress walked over, leashed me and led me out of the room. I have never been so wet and excited before in my life. It seemed as if the gallery was a million miles away. I could feel my heart beat harder and harder with every step. I never seen Mistress in heels like that before, but oh fuck, she worked it. I was proud to be her bitch and I was hell bent on making sure everyone knew that tonight.

The gallery was beautiful. I have been to galleries before, but never anything like this. I have never seen nor even heard of bondage art before. The total mind fuck was that I … we were part of it. We were actually considered part of the art on display. Mistress led me through the crowd. She had no concern for anyone there. She pushed her way through the crowd, with me in tow, forcing people to step out of our way. Mistress was so totally in control I didn't notice Mistress Kelly and Uwa. We crossed paths frequently, but my attention was totally on my Mistress.

Occasionally we would stop and Mistress would guide me into a pose and we would hold it until Mistress decided it was time for us to move on. People took photos of us with their cell phones. There was also a professional female photographer, taking photos for the gallery. I remember once Mistress put me on my hands and knees and had me go down so my forearms were flat on the ground and my ass was in the air. Mistress tapped my inner thighs with her riding crop until I spread my legs as far as they would go. She knelt down next to me and spread my ass so far apart my asshole and pussy lips parted. She leaned so far forward I could feel her hair resting the small of my back and on the top of my ass. I could feel the juices slowly drip from me as the shutter and flash from the photographer's camera went off behind me.

Not once that evening did Mistress strike me with her crop, spank me or even yell at me. She guided me with a gentle hand that entire evening. Yet I felt totally dominated by her. It was unlike anything I ever felt before in my entire life. In many ways it was more intense and definitely more erotic then if she had used the crop on me. But the most erotic part of the evening is when Mistress fed me chocolate dipped strawberries and Champaign as the photographer photographed us. It was so intimate I didn't even notice the flash from her camera.

The most frustrating part of the evening came near the end. Mistress put on this huge red leather strap on. We stood in the middle of the room. Mistress lifted my left leg up until I was on my tip toes. She pulled me as close to her as I would go. She looked directly in my eyes. We were so close I could feel her breath, but our lips never touched. I could feel the tip of her strap on brushing ever so lightly against my clit and occasionally slipping just barely between my pussy lips, but never penetrating me. I so wanted Mistress to fuck me hard and long right there. I didn't care who was looking. But she didn't. She knew I was close to orgasm. She whispered to me, "I forbid you to cum."

I was so on the edge not only did my voice quiver, but my entire body quivered as I responded with a whisper, "Yes Mistress."

I was so frustrated a single tear ran down my left cheek. As the photographer's flash exploded in my face I heard her utter, "beautiful ... perfection."

Afterwards Mistress placed me in a steel cage which had wheels and a handle attached to it. My hands and legs were latched to rings on each corner of the cage. Mistress didn't pull me around for the rest of the evening. There were times she left me alone. I could see her watching not too far away. But I was completely helpless and exposed to the onlookers. No one touched me, or the cage. But somehow I felt crowded. I could feel myself almost panic every time I lost sight of Mistress. But she never stayed out of sight for too long.

The gallery showing was over just a little after two in the morning. Master Scott called Mistress Yvonne and Mistress Kelly over to the side. Uwa came over to my cage. I thought he would let me out, but he didn't. He somehow was allowed to wear his body suit for the entire evening.

After Master Scott walked away, Mistress Kelly motioned for Uwa. Uwa picked up the handle to my cage and pulled me with him in tow. He followed our Mistresses as they walked out the front door and outside. Yes it was late and the only people out were those who were leaving the gallery, but I was so scared someone would see us. I mean I was completely naked in a cage. We went about three blocks to a house. Mistress Yvonne unlocked the door and Uwa wheeled me inside and locked the door behind us.

Mistress Kelly and Uwa went into one room. Mistress Yvonne wheeled me into another room. She didn't say a word to me. For some reason I was so compliant that evening I didn't even think to speak unless first spoken to. Once inside the room, Mistress unlatched and then re-latched my arms and legs so I could lie down. The bottom of the cage was cold and Mistress didn't give me a blanket or pillow for the night.

Mistress undressed where I could see her. She turned down the bed. She walked over and turned out the lights. I could see her silhouette as she passed in front of the moon lit curtains and climbed into bed for the night.

I didn't sleep much that night. I was way too horny and there was nothing I could do about it. All I could do was fantasize about being taken by Mistress. All the good that did was to frustrate me even more. Yet I never felt so close to Mistress in all the time I have known her.

I wasn't sure if it was sure if it was me who was changing or if it was Mistress who had changed. Or maybe we were both changing. All I know is things were different. I felt as if she was a part of me. I don't know how to explain it, but it felt right.

I awaken the next morning by the rattling sounds of Uwa releasing me from my cage. Mistress' bed was made and she was nowhere to be found. The cloths I arrived in, minus the granny panties, were laid out for me on the bed.

"Where is Mistress?" I asked as I crawled out of my cage and slowly stretched.

"Our Mistresses returned to the Mansion. I made us breakfast. I will drive us back afterwards."

"Where are my panties?" I asked as I looked over my outfit.

"I ripped them up and threw them out." He replied in his usual superior tone.

Somehow my skirt seemed a bit shorter without panties. Of course Uwa adjusted my cloths as I dressed. I finally just gave in and allowed him to dress me.

Her Bitch or His

As soon as we returned to the Mansion I headed for the shower. I wanted to freshen up before I went looking for Mistress. I love the showers here there is always plenty of hot water. I usually take long showers, but I was too excited. When I stepped out of the shower, Elyse was standing there and handed me a towel.

"We have a class in ten minutes, in the lower dungeons" She said.

"It's Saturday, we don't have classes on the weekends." I wiped the water from my face, "What the fuck are you wearing?" She was wearing a grey dress about which was loose fitting and came down mid-thigh. It looked like a prison uniform.

"I know it's hideous. Yours is on your bed. Today is a special mandatory class."

"I was hoping to spend time with Mistress."

Elyse took the towel from me as I was starting to dry my hair. "All of the head Mistresses are gone for the weekend. I heard they were going to some sort of seminar. The Dungeon Masters and Mistresses are in charge until they return." She stepped to the side and motioned for me to leave. She gave my ass a smack as I passed.

"What the fuck!" It stung like hell. My ass was still damp.

She chuckled, "Sorry. I couldn't resist."

I walked over to my bed and slipped on the dress. I started for the closet to slip on a pair of shoes.

Elyse took me by my arm and pulled me out of the room. "Come on Babe Gurl no shoes, bras or panties allowed in the lower dungeon. Besides we have three minutes."

"Why bother with clothing at all?" I really wasn't asking a question. I was mostly venting my sexual frustration. All I could think about was the next time I will be able to spend time alone with my Mistress, which may not be until next weekend.

We arrived at the lower dungeon just as they were about to close the door. We spotted Justine kneeling next to Uwa. We went over and knelt down next to them. We were not arranged in any particular order. That was fine with me. I was getting a bit tired of being the center of attention. We startled Justine when we knelt next to her. She was too busy flirting with Uwa to notice us enter.

The men uniforms were even more hideous than ours. It was the same drab grey. You know those old black and white silent movies? They had those old one piece swimsuits for men. They were like those, only skin tight and showed everything.

Master Dwain, one of the Dungeon Masters in training, stood in front of us. "Today we are going to go over the proper care and maintenance of a dungeon and equipment. Every Master and Mistress will have their personal equipment. It is the responsibility of their submissive to properly care for them. It is also your responsibility to maintain the dungeon and its equipment as well."

Mistress Cleo, I hate that name…Mistress Cleo another trainee. She's a real bitch. I really hate her. She cut me off in the hallway once and almost knocked me over, when she bumped into me. She had the nerve to demand an apology from me.

Anyway, Mistress Cleo walked up next to Master Dwain and placed a duffle bag she was carrying next to him. She opened it up and removed a bamboo cane.

"We'll start with the cane", Mistress Cleo stated. "If you allow the cane to dry out it will become brittle and break. It shows a lack of respect for your Master or Mistress and their equipment if you don't properly care for it. One way to prolong the life of a cane is to cut the ends and allow it to stand in a container of water."

The class wasn't as boring as I thought it would be. There were a lot of hands on training. We were each given a duffle bag identical to the one Mistress Cleo had. I never held a bull whip before. It was heavier that I thought. The sight of it scared me. But Elyse

97

caressed and handled it as if she wanted to make love to it. She knew exactly how to handle and care for it.

At the end of the day I took the duffle bag to Mistress' room. I slept there that night, in case she returned. I didn't sleep in the bed. I slept on the floor, completely nude, at the foot of the bed.

I didn't hear her enter and her bed was untouched, but when I awoke there was a single red rose next to me. I looked but Mistress was nowhere to be found. I even looked in our private dungeon. I placed the duffle bag in our dungeon. I showered and put back on my slave dress and returned to the dorm.

We spent the rest of the day cleaning the dungeon and the equipment. The scrubbing of the floors I could have done without, but it was fun when we got to the equipment, many of the equipment I never seen before such as the Saint Andrew Cross. It was basically a large wooden X. But Master Dwain and Mistress Cleo demonstrated how all of the furniture and equipment worked.

Master Dwain pointed to his female submissive. She stood up and walked over to him. He stripped her completely nude. Mistress Cleo handed Master Dwain a long thick rope. Although I watched closely I could not tell you how he did it. He tied the rope around her body so it actually looked like a body harness. It even had three diamond shapes going up her stomach. He wrapped her nipples so tight they actually turned red. He then tied her to the Saint Andrew Cross.

Mistress Cleo took two chains with clamps on each end and held them up for us to see. She attached one end to her right nipple and the other to her left pussy lip. She adjusted the clamps and tugged on the chain to ensure the clamps were tight. She did the same to the girls left nipple and right pussy lip. She then adjusted the length of the chains until the girls pussy was pulled open.

Master Dwain slowly turned the cross until she was completely upside down. I was amazed to see that the Saint Andrew Cross actually rotated. He then removed a riding crop from his duffle bag and started taunting her with it. He wasn't hitting her hard. He was barely tapping her inner thighs and her exposed pussy. He brought her to the edge of orgasm and then he stopped. He just left her there tied to that cross upside down. I could feel her frustration and see it on her face. She was breathing heavily, red face was red and her breasts had begun to turn purple.

He left her there for a good ten minutes, before letting her down. She gasped deeply as he released each clamp. You could see the teeth marks from the clamps embedded deep in her milky white skin. The ropes left its marks embedded deep within her skin as well. Her breast quickly turned from purple to a deep red, except for the area covered by the rope it was pale white.

Her legs were so shaky she collapsed to her knees and pleaded to Master Dwain to allow her to cum. At first it seemed that her pleas fell on empty ears. After about a minute or so, he turned and nodded yes, granting her request. She spread her legs; lend back and started masturbating with one hand and rubbing her nipples with the other hand. She worked herself into frenzy until she collapsed in an explosion of ecstasy. It was the hottest thing I ever saw. She made me wet just watching.

After dinner I went to bed at the dorm. I missed my Mistress. I wore my favorite cotton pajamas. There is nothing sexy about them. They are yellow with brown bunnies. No they are not the ones with the feet. It is a regular blouse and pants set.

Everyone else was out by the pool. Just as I was about to go to sleep, there was a knock at my door. It startled me. No one knocks around here. The doors are always unlocked, unless one of the moderators locks it.

I sat up and called out, "Who is it?"

I heard a male voice answer, but I couldn't make out the response. Maybe I wasn't completely awake and didn't quite recognize the voice. So I got up and went to the door. I opened the door and there was Uwa standing there wearing only a pair of Speedos. "What are you doing here I asked?" I know that sounds kind of rude, but I was still half asleep.

He didn't wait for an invitation, he just walked in. I had to take a few steps back. He closed the door behind him. "Why aren't you out there where all of the action is?" He walked over and sat at the edge of my bed. He motioned for me and patted the bed next to him. "You look troubled, tell me about it."

I climbed into bed and sat next to him. I crossed my legs and pulled my knees to my chest. "Nothing is wrong. I'm just tired."

He just sat there and stared at me. He didn't say anything he just sat there looking at me. The silence was driving me crazy, so I had to say something. "I miss my Mistress. I'm not use to this type of treatment."

"Is she being too rough on you?"

"No that not it. The fact is that I like it. I'm just use to having her all to myself."

He placed his hand on my knee and caressed it slowly. "Are things moving a little too fast for you?"

"Yeah", I answered in a surprisingly soft voice. I don't know why but I was on the verge of tears. "I like most of the changes. But I miss having her to myself."

He responded with a half-smile. "You are a spoiled princess Babe Gurl. You will see that you still have your Mistress. But she has responsibilities in accordance with her position, as do you." He reached up and moved my hair away from my face. "Both your Mistress and you have a decision to make, before this is over. Just remember, there is no right or wrong answer."

I hate being a girl sometimes. The tears started flowing and I couldn't stop them. "What if there is a right or wrong answer and I choose wrong? What if I mess it all up?"

"Sara McNeil, what am I to do with you?"

"Love me." Oh fuck! I don't know why I just said that. It just slipped out.

He caressed my face with both hand, very gently. I opened my mouth to say something cleaver. Not that I had anything cleaver to say. It was at that moment he kissed me, firmly on my lips. He was an excellent kisser. He wiped away my tears with his thumbs.

I knew it was wrong and I should have stopped it right then and there, but I didn't. I just let it happen. He slowly unbuttoned my blouse as he kissed down my neck. He removed my blouse and tossed it to the side. He pushed me back on the bed and made his way to my breast. My entire breast fit in his mouth.

I pushed him back. "I can't. I'm sorry. I can't have sex with you."

I felt his hands slip into my waistband. "This isn't sex Sara McNeil." He pulled my pants off and tossed them on the other side of the room. "This is me eating your sweet pussy until you cum."

I wasn't quite sure of the difference. But that was the end of my resistance. He pulled my legs apart, knelt between them and pulled me to him and tossed my legs over his shoulders.

He took his time, kissing my inner thigh. It didn't take long for me to get wet. He parted my lips slightly and allowed his tongue to slightly invade me. I instinctively arched my back, causing his entire tongue to enter me. My legs tightened around his neck. He reached under my back and stood up, taking me with him. He held me in place by my ass and buried his face between my thighs. I balanced myself by holding onto his head.

Then he did something I didn't expect. He started teasing my pee hole with his tongue. My stomach went weak. When the tip of his tongue entered my pee hole I had an overwhelming urge to pee. How embarrassing. I wanted to die. I'm just glad my bladder was mostly empty. It was a short but steady stream. It didn't detour Uwa in the least. He immediately attacked my clit. I never cum and peed at the same time, but it was very intense. I didn't think I had enough pee inside of me to pee twice. It was so intense I almost blacked out.

He lowered me back onto the bed as he licked my pussy clean. He tucked me in and gave me a goodnight kiss. "You are a spoiled little princess, Sara McNeil. But you are still my Babe Gurl."

I was asleep a few minutes after he left. I don't know what choices I would have to make, but it didn't matter, at least not that night.

The next morning when I awoke, I sort of laid there for a while. I wasn't sure if it was all a dream or real. Since I was lying in bed completely naked, I sort of figured it really happened.

Elyse came out of the bathroom wrapped in a towel and drying her hair. "Where did Justine go?"

"I don't know. I just woke up."

"She wanted to shower next. If I were you I would go for it before she gets back."

Just as I was getting out of the bed, the door opened. Elyse and I screamed and jumped up on our beds. A five foot cat pounced into our room.

After a few seconds Elyse jumps off the bed and runs towards it jumping with joy, "Kazumi!"

"What the fuck?" I had no clue as to what was going on. All I knew is that some freak in a giant cat suit was bouncing up and down with a naked Elyse.

Elyse gave me that duh look, "Kazumi ... Justine's neko name."

Justine immediately went into a ta-da stance. I have to admit she looked sort of cute, scary but cute. She was a black and white cat. It was actually a furry costume, with fur and everything. She even had a cat nose and mouth, paws and a tail. The costume covered everything except her crotch and the center half of her ass.

Anyway, Justine ... I mean Kazumi didn't talk. I guess it is some sort of furry rule or code. She motioned to her collar. Elyse saw a note stuck under Kazumi's collar. She removed it and read it.

"They don't want us to dress. We are to go to breakfast nude and then go straight to the lower dungeon."

I took a quick shower and we left for breakfast. It was a little strange walking down the halls with a giant ultra-hyper cat. The things I do for my friends.

During breakfast Justine refused to remove her snout. So Mistress Kim shoved bits of food through an opening on her snout. That wasn't the freaky part. There were about six other furry people (I guess that's what you call them) in the room. Two of them were Dominates. Until this morning I was beginning to really respect Master Samuel. Now all I will see when I look at him is a giant gerbil. I'm not quite sure what he was actually supposed to be.

After breakfast we went to the lower dungeon. But I got side tracked when I saw my Mistress go into Master Adam's office. I don't know why, but when I saw the door didn't close completely I walked over to sneak a peek. I didn't like what I saw.

Mistress Julie had stripped my Mistress nude and forced her to kneel in front of Master Adams. Mistress Julie pulled my Mistress hair back forcing her to look up at Master Adams. I had to get close to hear wheat was being said.

Looking down at my Mistress Master Adams spoke to my Mistress, "I'm disappointed in you. I'm beginning to doubt you have what it takes to run this Mansion or even be a Mistress."

Then I saw something that really got me angry. My Mistress started pleading with that fat cow who calls himself a Master. "I can do this I promise you. Just give me a chance to prove myself."

Master Adams continued, "You have a natural submissive and you are letting her slip through your fingers because you can't commit."

"I can commit. I am committed," Mistress Yvonne responded.

"I don't see it," Master Adams responded.

Mistress Julie added her two cents. "You are too easy on her. It's as if you're afraid to let go. I'm not sure if you don't trust yourself or you are afraid of losing her."

"She's a novice. I don't want to scare her off," Mistress Yvonne added.

As much as I hate to admit it Mistress Julie actually said something I sort of agreed with. "She maybe a novice, but you will only lose her if you hold back. She needs more. She needs a Mistress who isn't afraid to use her totally and completely. Or maybe we should find a Master for her?"

Not that I would ever want neither another Mistress nor a Master, but I do sometimes wish Mistress would use me more. Sometimes she takes me right to the edge and then backs off. But I don't see how that is any of their business.

"I'm going to give you one last chance," Master Adams pronounced. "Here is how it's going to work."

Before I could hear anymore, Elyse grabbed me by my arm and pulled me away from the door and halfway down the hall. "What in the hell do you think you are doing?" She asked.

"You are hurting me." I pulled my arm free. She was clinching me so tight she left a bright red handprint. "Did you see how they are treating Mistress? They have no right."

"They have the right to do whatever they want. They run all of this." Elyse can be a self-righteous bitch sometimes, but this wasn't one of those times. I guess she was right. "I don't know what you saw or heard and I don't care. You owe it to your Mistress to serve her to the best of your ability. You need to either commit to her or let her move on."

"I am committed to Mistress." I was a bit offended by her remarks.

"Where you committed to her committed to your Mistress last night when you fucked Uwa?"

I almost chocked on my own heart. "I didn't fuck Uwa."

"I don't care what you do, but you need to be a little more discrete. I walked in on you last night. You were too busy riding Uwa's face neither of you saw me. I immediately left and came back a few hours, you were asleep." Elyse moved a stray hair from my face, "Look all I'm saying is not to waste your time on Uwa. He is a switch. Unless you are willing to dominate him or share him with Kelly, who is also a switch, it will never work."

"What's a switch?" I have heard that word used before, but I was always too embarrassed to ask. I don't know why I chose now to ask.

"A switch is someone who is a Dominate part of the time and a submissive at other times.

"So, Uwa dominates Mistress Kelly?"

"Yes."

As usual I was confused. "I thought this was a dungeon was run entirely by Mistresses?"

"It is. What they do in their free time is no one's business but theirs."

I was still a bit confused, but I wanted to set the record straight concerning Uwa and me. "I don't know what you think, but Uwa and I are just friends. What happened last night was a mistake and it will never happen again. I don't know why I let it happen. It was a stupid thing to do."

"Trust me. Uwa is not your friend. He is a user. You are just another notch on his belt."

"I wasn't aware you knew him so well."

"I don't. I know of him. But there are others who know him very well."

"I told you it was a mistake."

"Look, I'm not going to tell your Mistress or anything like that. It is really none of my business. I consider us friends and I don't want to see you get hurt. Sooner or later you will have to commit one way or the other."

"I am committed to my Mistress. This is all just happening so fast and I got carried away. I missed my Mistress and he just showed up and I let things go too far." I wanted to find a hole and fall into it. Once again I betrayed my Mistress and myself.

Elyse held my hands. "I'm not judging. We've fucked around some and I've fucked around with a few of the other submissive females. I know for a fact Justine is hot for Uwa. You just have to be honest with yourself."

Just then Mistress Yvonne exited Master Adams' office escorted by Mistress Julie towards the lower dungeon. I didn't see my Mistress face, but she looked sad to me. It made me angry. I started to go towards them, but Elyse pulled me back towards her.

Elyse squeezed my hands slightly. "What in the hell do you think you are doing?"

I was furious. "I don't like the way they are treating her."

"How do you think they will treat her if her submissive runs to her rescue? She will never be able to show her face again. You had best learn your place, for your sake and the sake of your Mistress."

I knew Elyse was right. There was no way I could run to her rescue. All I could do was to watch as they turned the corner.

I was about to follow when Elyse pulled me back and pushed my back to the wall. "You know what you are Sara McNeil? You are spoiled and selfish. You wiggle your ass and flash your smile and you expect the world to fall at your feet. You are playing games with your Mistress and you need to stop."

Who in the hell does this bitch think she is? "I love my Mistress and I'm not playing games with her. I made a mistake. I told you it will not happen again." I started to cry.

Elyse slapped my face so hard she almost knocked me to the ground. She yanked me by my arm and pushed me back against the wall. "You stop it! You stop it right now! Don't you dare shed those crocodile tears in front of me."

I was in total shock. I wasn't expecting that. My left check was on fire. It felt as if a thousand bees stung me all at once. I was afraid that if I raised my hand to rub my check she would just slap me again. I did my best to hold back the tears. My entire body was shaking.

Elyse grabbed my chin with her left hand and lifted my head and looked me square in the eye. "This is how it's going to be Babe Gurl. Whatever it is you are doing with Uwa or not doing with him, it ends today. If I even think you are fucking around with him or any man without your Mistress approval, I will paddle your ass raw. Do you understand me?"

"You're not my Mistress." I could feel my heart beating in my throat as I choked those words out.

She squeezed my chin even harder. "You're right I am not your Mistress. But as long as you are here I am your sister, your big sister. You will learn your place."

"How in the fuck am I at the bottom, when my Mistress is at the top?"

"Your Mistress earned her position, just as you earned yours." She stuck her right index finger in my face. "If you cuss at me one more time I am going to drag you into the washroom and wash your mouth with soap. Are we clear?"

Looking back I should have just said yes. "Justine and I were here first. Who in the fuck made you the boss?"

Elyse didn't answer. True to her word she grabbed me by my arm and pulled me to the washroom. I tried to resist, but she was too determined. She took me to the corner wash basin and pushed me in front of it. She turned on the water and ran it over her right hand. Then she squired some liquid soap in her hand and used her fingers to work it up into lather.

107

"Open your mouth," she ordered.

I took a step back.

She pulled me back into place and grabbed a handful of my hair. "Babe Gurl, don't make me tell you again."

I slowly complied. As soon as I parted my lips, she shoved her soapy hand in my mouth and started scrubbing my tongue, then the inside of my checks and then the roof of my mouth. I gagged and chocked.

I leaned forward to spit out some of the soap. Elyse pulled my head back by my hair. "Don't you dare, I will tell you when you can spit." She placed her right hand under the running water and added more soap. "Open up," she ordered. This time she didn't wait for me to open my mouth. She shoved her hand in my mouth and washed my mouth out until suds were spilling out and running down my throat.

She made me hold the suds in my mouth for about a minute. I was on the verge of puking when she allowed me to rinse. I must have rinsed furiously for five minutes and I could still taste the soap in my mouth.

Elyse pulled me up and hugged me. Then she pulled back and looked me in the face. "I don't want to be this way with you. We are going to be here for a long time. I know you love your Mistress, but I know Uwa. Uwa and Kelly collect slaves. They get a thrill out of stealing slaves from their Masters and Mistresses. When they are tired of them they simply dismiss them."

"I was such a fool." I know she told me not to cry, but I couldn't help myself.

"You are not a fool Sara. You are just our Babe Gurl and Justine and I will just have to look after you."

How she can go from a ragging bitch one minute to someone I want to curl up with is a mystery to me. She washed my face and we walked back to the dungeon.

When we entered the dungeon I could tell from her stance my Mistress was in full bitch mode. She was dressed in this skin tight red rubber body suit. She wore red full length nylons with red lacy garter belt. She wore red knee high Dominatrix boots. She had a red riding crop in her hand. Mistress Kimberly and Mistress Robyn stood on either sides of her. Both were dressed identically to Mistress Yvonne.

There was a cart with what looked like a couple of costumes on it and some other stuff. I didn't get a chance to look at them. Mistress had me kneel in front of the cart and look straight ahead. Elyse knelt next to me and Justine knelt next to Elyse. Justine was still dressed as Kazumi.

Mistress Julie walked in. "Today we are going to cover role playing. Our cliental covers a wide range of fetishes. Role playing is amongst the most popular. The main thing to remember is not to break character." She points to Justine. "Kazumi is what is known as a furry. Most furry will arrive in character. This is a very personal persona and is to be respected. Kazumi is a cat girl, also known as a neko."

Mistress Julie looks over at Mistress Robyn. Mistress Robyn removes one of the costumes from the cart and holds it up. Mistress Julie continues, "Mistress Robyn is holding up a puppy suit. They also come in what's known as kitten suits as well. Elyse isn't a pet, but we are going to use her to demonstrate how the suit goes on."

They stood Elyse up and she stepped into the costume. It was complete with paws, but no tail. To me it looked a lot like the furry suit Justine was wearing, except it wasn't as detailed. She looked sort of like a Dalmatian. Next they put a hood on her with dog ears attached to it. They gave her a snout with an O-ring built inside of it. It held her mouth open. When she stuck her tongue out it looked like she was panting. She also started to drool after a while. Finally they lubricated Elyse's asshole and slowly worked a butt plug with a tail made onto her. When the finished dressing her they made her kneel down on her hands and knees. She didn't look too happy or comfortable.

Mistress Julie continued, "Submissive pets may or may not wear a costume. It is a decision made between them and their Master or Mistress. Regardless if they are in costume or not, if the submissive is a pet then they are to be treated as such."

Mistress Yvonne picked up the other suit. She cut off Mistress Julie in midsentence. "This is a Punishment suit, also known as a Bitch suit. Sara is neither a Furry nor a pet. She is my bitch and she deserves punishment." Mistress Yvonne looked down at me, "On your back bitch and get those knees up."

I did as I was instructed. I was almost in a panic. What if she knew about Uwa? I couldn't think of any other reason I had done to deserve punishment.

Mistress started by slipping the suit over my two bent knees. The fit was tight. It forced my heels against my upper thighs. The suit was pulled up over my ass and pulled snug.

"Bend your elbows," Mistress Yvonne ordered.

Mistress slipped the suit over my bent arms forcing my hands to my shoulders. There was a hood attached to the suit which was slipped over my head. It also had a built in O-ring which forced my mouth opened. I could still taste the soap.

Mistress rolled me over so that I was on my knees and elbow. The suit was well padded. Mistress zipped the suit up. She lubricated my asshole and slowly worked one of those butt plug tails inside of me. Mistress placed a collar and leash around my neck.

Mistress walked me around the dungeon. It took a while. I couldn't go very fast. It was very awkward. That butt plug didn't help. The tail attached to it weighed it down. Every time I went too slow Mistress' crop came down across the exposed part of my ass. She sometimes smacked my pussy. The first time I thought it was an accident. After the third time, I knew Mistress wasn't that careless.

Mistress Yvonne continued her lecture as she paraded me through the dungeon. "As you can see you can't keep them in this suit too long. Their circulation can get cut off. I wouldn't leave your submissive in this suit longer than thirty to forty-five minutes to begin with. Remember this is a punishment suit. It isn't meant for long term use."

Mistress stopped me right in the middle of everyone. She spread my pussy apart. "As you can see my bitch is also a little slut who loves humiliation. Look at how wet she is."

I don't know where she got it from, but I felt a rubber dildo slide deep inside of me. At first she started slowly, working it in and out of me slightly. Then she started twisting it slightly. The more I moaned with pleasure the faster and deeper she fucked me. It pushed against the butt plug in my ass."

Mistress saw I was close to orgasm. "Don't you dare … You fucking little whore, don't you dare cum without my permission." The problem is that my Mistress knows exactly where my spot is and she made sure to hit it often.

Mistress Julie walked over and lifted my head up by my hair. I was drooling like crazy. "Give her to Uwa. Let him fuck her. Look at her you know she wants him."

Oh fuck! They know. I fucked everything up.

Mistress Yvonne grabbed my hair way from Mistress Julie. Fuck that hurt. It felt as if I was in the middle of a cat fight. "I don't care who she wants. This is my bitch and I decide who she fucks and who fucks her."

"She already fucked him," Mistress Julie taunted.

I could feel my heart in my throat. I wanted to disappear.

"I know," Mistress Yvonne responded. "I sent him to her. Like I said she is my bitch and I say who fucks her or not."

What the fuck! I wasn't expecting to hear that.

Mistress continued, "I will punish my slutty bitch for her failure." She pulled the dildo out of me and slid it into my mouth and started face fucking me with it as she tapped my exposed clit with her ridding crop. That suit held me in place and prevented me from moving away from her crop. I gagged on the dildo as it slid in and out of my throat, never leaving my mouth. I could taste the soap as the suds foamed up in my mouth as it mixed with my saliva.

It was humiliating and embarrassing and I loved every second of it. Mistress didn't allow me to cum. As hard as it was, I managed to control myself. Mistress led me out of the dungeon and back to my room where she removed the bitch suit. She didn't say anything to me. She just took the suit and left.

I laid there on the bed. I was so confused. My Mistress sent Uwa to me as a test and I failed. Maybe Uwa was right? Maybe I am a spoiled bratty princess? I deserved to be treated like a slutty whore by Elyse. She's right, I haven't earned my position. All I did was abuse my Mistress love and trust.

Because my Mistress is away I stray like some slut whore. I don't deserve her. I wouldn't blame her if she dumped my sorry ass. I don't care about any of this. I just want her.

The suds in my mouth had turned to a paste and had dried in my mouth. I jumped up and ran into the washbasin and started rinsing my mouth. The more I rinsed the more suds formed in my mouth. I really hated Elyse at this point. I finally rinsed all of the suds out of my mouth, although the taste of soap was still there.

I didn't bother to get dressed. I walked to my bed and flopped face down on it. I really fucked up. Now I fear it is out of my hands. All I could do was curl up and cry myself to sleep.

Her Slut

I did my best to avoid Uwa for the rest week. Of course we had some contact and we did have to talk. But I tried my best to keep it short and to the point. It was hard. Uwa was as always quite the charmer. He is also quite forward at times. My Mistress kept a close eye on us. Elyse and Justine kept an eye on us as well.

Every time I saw my Mistress with Master Adams and Mistress Julie, my blood boiled. I could only imagine what they were saying and doing to her. But Elyse was correct. They only way I could help my Mistress were to become the submissive she deserved. The problem is I don't really know what type of submissive she wants. We never really talked about that.

It was Friday evening and I was excited. I finally will get some free time alone with my Mistress. After dinner I took a quick shower. I put on a blue oriental style dress Mistress seemed to like. It had a very detailed pattern on it. The dress was short and barely covered my ass. I had to take care when I bent over or sat down. Mistress didn't allow me to wear panties in our private room at the main Mansion. You ever tried walking up three flights of windy stairs dressed like a high priced Asian whore?

When I arrived Mistress Yvonne was nowhere to be found. There was however a note addressed to me.

> *Dear Slut,*
>
> *Strip and put your clothes away. Go to the center of the foyer. Assume the Nadu position. I will send someone to prepare you.*
>
> *Love, Mistress*

You know this sucks. I mean they give us all of these cute outfits and I spend most of my time walking around naked. I have a dresser full of panties I never wear. I stripped and put away my clothes as instructed. Something told me I would be waiting for a while. So I made myself a cheese sandwich. I was going to grill it, but then the place would smell like toast. I almost grilled it just to leave evidence.

After I finished my sandwich I went to the foyer and assumed the Nadu position. I hate Gorean Slave Positions. They are so ridged. I had to kneel there with my back straight and my ass on that cold wood floor, with my legs spread, head forward, with my eyes cast downward and my hands on my thighs with my palms upward. I sat there for at least an hour and a half. Good thing I ate that sandwich.

Finally the door opened. A rush of cold air turned my entire body into one big goose bump. Two masked men wearing black tank tops and black pants entered carrying a large workout bench. You know the ones in the gym the weightlifters use. It looked heavy. I wish they would have closed the door behind them. I was on display for every maid, butler and whoever just happened by, brilliant. A few minutes later they came back out and left. Of course they left the door open.

After about fifteen minutes they returned. They were each carrying a hug black duffle bag. One of the bags made a heavy clanking sound. That was scary. I heard them drop the bags and they came back out to the foyer. They each grabbed me under my arms and lifted me to my feet. They ushered me into the sitting room.

They didn't speak to me or each other. They sat me down on the edge of the weight bench. One man pulled a thick rope out of one of the duffle bags and tied my hands together in front of me, while the other man angled the bench up behind me about fifteen degrees. They laid me back. They placed one of those thick bars on the posts and tied my hands to it. They duck taped the bar in place. They tied the ropes around my ankles. They sort of looked like nooses. They lifted my legs up over my head by the ropes and tied them to the bar on either side of my hands.

They took out two additional ropes, looped them around my upper thigh and tied them to the legs. They then took two additional pieces and tied my elbows to my ankles. I was now completely immobile, helpless and completely exposed. Just when I thought

114

they were done. One of them started lubricating my exposed asshole, with some sort of oil. His finger was huge. It felt like a huge dildo being shoved up my ass. I was about to let out a moan when the other one placed one of those ball gags with holes in it into my mouth and buckled it tightly into place. While the one guy molested my ass as he lubed me up, the other one braided a rope into my hair and then tied the end of the rope to the bar forcing me to look forward at all times.

When they finished they stood back and admired their handy work. While one checked the ropes, the other checked the bench for sturdiness and adjusted the bench to support my back. Then they just left me there and turned out all of the lights. I heard the doors close and lock behind them. I'm just glad I didn't have anything to drink.

I lost track of time. I think I dozed off a few times. Finally, I heard someone enter the foyer. I heard familiar voices as they entered the sitting room. It took a few moments for my eyes to adjust once the lights came on. Mistress Yvonne had returned home with another Dungeon Mistress and her two female slaves. The two slaves were wearing thick black leather gags with long, thick black dildos attached to them. They were both completely nude except for a collar and one of them wore black leather chastity belt which was locked with tiny heart shaped lock.

The slaves were lead in crawling on leashes to about two feet from the sofa. They were placed about a foot apart, one facing the sofa and one facing the opposite direction. The two masked men returned and balanced a glass coffee table top on their backs. A butler came out and set a silver tray on the coffee table. The tray had a silver coffee pot and two china coffee cups on it. It also had some sort of cake or cookies.

Mistress Yvonne and the other Mistress sat and talked for a while. Their conversation was sort of boring so I don't remember what it was about. After about twenty minutes or so my Mistress stood up and walked over to me. She asked the other Mistress, "Mistress Marie, have you met my slut?"

Mistress Marie answered, "I definitely know who she is, but I have never met her. I usually see that Uwa sniffing around her."

"Yes, I have to keep an eye on Uwa. But tonight I'm going to remind her that she belongs to me." Mistress Yvonne walked behind me and came back holding a metal briefcase. Where in the hell that thing came from? I have never seen it before. Mistress set the briefcase on the coffee table and opened it up.

Mistress Marie's voice filled with excitement, "I like your style."

Mistress removed several metal items from the briefcase. "You connect the wires and I'll get the slut ready.

I had no idea what Mistress had planned, but I didn't like that it involved wires. Nothing good can come from that.

Mistress inserted a metal butt plug in my ass. Because my ass was still well lubed, it went in fairly easy. It was heavy though. She attached two small metal clamps to my pussy lips. She ran the wire around my legs and pulled them taught so they kept my pussy lips spread apart. She then clamped another pair on each of my nipples. Mistress finished by clamping one to my clit. Mistress Marie walked over and attached wires to the end of the butt plug and all of the clamps.

Mistress Marie held up this thing, it looked like a curling iron, sort of. Only it had a glass tube at the end of it. "I think you should start with the wand." She turned it on. It started crackling and blue sparks filled the tube, like one of those static crystal ball things. She handed it to my Mistress.

My Mistress started slowly. She ran it ever so lightly across my tummy. It didn't hurt but it did tingle. It felt like tiny prickles. It caused my tummy to contract. Mistress ran it over my arms and legs as well. As she moved up my legs I could see that she wasn't touching me at all. There were tiny arches of electricity coming from the wand to my skin.

After a few moments Mistress turned off and put the wand down. Mistress then very lightly and slowly ran her finger nails all over my body. She barely touched me. It drove me crazy. That wand thing must have made me hyper sensitive. She brought me to the point of orgasm and then stopped.

I was in a sexual frenzy. Without warning a mild electrical shock came from the butt plug and ran throughout my entire body. I convulsed, but the ropes held me securely in place. Then after a few second another burst ran from my nipples and really set me off. I had a full on orgasm. Of course Mistress noticed.

Mistress leaned over and stuck her fingers in my pussy and pulled it out. "Look at this little slut. She has no self-control." Mistress slowly sucked her finger clean.

In a series of short bursts Mistress Marie sent short jolts to my pussy lips and clit. I never felt anything like this before. It was like my senses were on overload. She gave me a few seconds break and then she stepped it up a notch. There must have been a random setting on that thing. A series of random bursts or various degrees of intensity ran through my body. I screamed, not in pain, but ecstasy. It's hard to explain. It did hurt some, especially my clit. But it was a real turn on for me.

I must have passed out. But it didn't feel as if I passed out. I sort of remember all of it, except it felt as if I wasn't really there at one point. It was as if I was in another place, almost like a blitz. I don't remember being untied and having my gag removed. But there I was sipping water through a straw from a glass being held by my Mistress.

"Welcome back," Mistress Marie said to me. She then placed her hand on Mistress' shoulder. "We have to do this again."

"Definitely," Mistress Yvonne responded.

Mistress Marie led her two slaves out, followed by the two masked men. Mistress Yvonne put the glass down and helped me up to my feet. At first I thought she was being a bit too fussy. But once I stood up my legs went weak. It took me a while get my legs back, but Mistress helped me to our room and into bed. I didn't feel sleepy but I fell asleep almost as soon as Mistress pulled the covers over me.

I woke up next to Mistress. It felt good to be in bed with her again. I laid there for a while just looking at her. I lifted to sheets and peaked under them. Mistress usually sleeps in the nude. I love looking at her tight ass. I wanted to wake her up, but she looked so peaceful. So I got up.

It was nice and warm so I only put on a black lingerie top with pink lace trim and pink pinstripes. I also put on a pair of pink panties. I also put my hair up in pigtails. I walked into the sitting room. The weight bench was gone. I was going to sit down, but I noticed a door I never seen before. I'm sure it was always there, but I don't spend much time in the sitting room. Until last night it always seemed like a rather boring place.

I walked in and to my surprise it was an exact replica of our old room, right down to the awful blankets and curtains. I don't know why, but I felt safe. I looked around and I found my favorite acrylic dildo.

Mistress' voice startled me, "Do you like?"

I don't know why but I panicked and hid the dildo under the pillow. I don't know why but I felt guilty. I turned around to see Mistress looking at me through a camcorder.

"Master Adams added it. He felt it would be a safe place for our private time together," Mistress explained.

"So this is like a free zone," I asked.

"No Mistress, no slave … just us."

I crawled onto the bed. "I am always your slut and you are always my Mistress." I started caressing my body, taunting Mistress with every movement. I spread my legs and rubbed my legs. I turned over onto my hands and knees and rubbed my ass looking back over my shoulders. I slowly pulled my top off and played with my

118

breasts. Mistress never complained, but I wish I had larger breasts. I mean a C cup would be nice.

I unlashed my panties and let them fall open. I slowly played with my clit. I reached back under the pillow and moistened the dildo in my mouth. It slid effortlessly inside my pussy. The notches on the dildo increased in size and felt even better when I pulled it out than it did when I pushed it in. I sped up at times but I had to slow down so not to cum too quickly. At times I forgot Mistress was there. I teased her by sucking and licking the dildo clean.

I guess I finally got to Mistress. She turned off the camcorder and crawled up between my legs. She licked my stomach and my breast. It tickled. We shared the wettest and most passionate kiss we have had in a long time. Mistress crawled up and positioned her sweet pussy right over me and lowered herself down onto my face.

I held her tightly in position by her hips. The more she grinded her hips the tighter I held her. At first I kissed her mound and then used my tongue to invade her. The closer she came to orgasm the more I concentrated my efforts on her clit. I knew I had her when I felt her entire body begin to quiver. I love the sounds she makes. She whimpers just before her orgasms, sweet music to my ears. I don't know why, but I cried a little at that moment.

I licked my lips clean as Mistress collapsed back onto the bed. I lie on top of her and rest my head on her breasts. Her breasts aren't much larger than mine, but they are perfect.

I watched as she fell asleep. She looked so happy and peaceful. She smiles in her sleep. I like the smell of her skin and her hair. I watched her breasts rise and fall with each breath as I fell asleep.

The Sting of Her Whip

We slept in each other's arms until noon that day. I woke up first and just laid still listening to the sound of Mistress' heart beat as her chest slowly rose and fell in a steady rhythm. I got up without waking her and took a long bath. I mainly just soaked. I usually take a bubble bath, but this time I used bath oil.

When I got out I dried off and wrapped a towel around myself and walked back to our main bedroom to dress. I wasn't sure what else if anything Mistress had planned for me today, so I just slipped on a pair of pink French cut panties, my collar and a pair of cut off jean that barely covered the little bit of ass I have and a blue tank top. I slipped on a pair of flip-flops and headed back to the other room.

I opened the door to find the maid making the bed. I gave a quick look around and then asked, "Have you seen Mistress Yvonne?"

The maid shrugged her shoulders. "Mistress Yvonne said she would be back in about twenty minutes."

"You know, I have seen you around and spoken to you several times in the past and I have never asked your name." I stated to the maid as she continued about her work.

"My name is Maria," she answered.

"Hello Maria. My name is Sara."

"I know who you are," she responded almost as if I were bothering her.

"Hopefully we will find some time to get to know each other better soon."

Maria asked, "Do you have anything you need washed? I'm about to do the laundry"

"No, I placed everything in the hamper. How do you like working here?"

She didn't respond. She just sort of rolled her eyes and kept working. So I left. What a bitch. I went into the small kitchen and made some a couple of eggs and toast. I never had brown eggs before. I don't know the difference, except for the color of the shell. I guess eggs are eggs.

After I ate I went and watched cartoons. Nothing else was on. Maria just sort of cleaned around me. I ignored her. Normally I would have offered to help.

When Mistress returned home, about an hour past when Maria said she would return; Maria became little Miss Chatter Box. "Hello Mistress Yvonne. I'll take those for you. If you're hungry I can make breakfast." She is such a kiss ass.

Mistress responded, "Thanks. I'm fine Maria. I ate already. Where is Sara?"

"She's just sitting around watching cartoons."

She is such a condescending bitch.

Mistress came in to the sitting room and picked up the remote and turned off the television. She slipped her index finger in the ring on my collar pulled me up to my feet. She didn't say a word. She led me to the door and removed a leash from the rack, leashed me and led me out the door. When we got to the floor below us, Mistress Kimberly and Mistress Robyn met us with Justine and Elyse in tow. They led us to a private dungeon in the lower level of the Mansion. I never knew this part of the Mansion existed.

They led us to the center of the dungeon and unleashed us. They ordered us to undress. It was cold. I got goose bumps. Mistress Kimberly comes back with this thick metal hook thing. It was like chrome and had a loop at the top end and three hooks evenly spaced. It looked heavy.

A loud clanking sound came from over our head. It caught me off guard and startled all of us. Someone was lowering a huge chain on some pulleys with chains dangling from them. Mistress Kimberly fastened the hook to the center chain. She then slipped one of the hooks into Justine's pussy and pulled Elyse so she was

121

facing Justine but turned slightly to the right and slipped the hook into her pussy as well. I was then called over and she did the same to me.

Mistress Robyn tied a rope around each of our waists and tied us so we were facing each other. Mistress Yvonne placed suspension cuffs on us and connected each of our hands to one of the chains above us. The chains were adjusted so that our hips were at equal height. I was on my tiptoes. The chain on the hook was adjusted so it fit snug on all of us. We were then hoisted off our feet. I don't know how far up we were, but it really didn't matter, my feet were off the ground and it felt as if we were at least twenty feet off the ground. In reality we were most likely only about a couple of inches or so off the ground.

They turned out the lights and left us dangling there. About fifteen minutes later the lights came back on. Our Mistresses returned. They were dressed in matching black latex body suits with knee high latex boots and full-length latex gloves. They were also carrying these long ass bullwhips and were accompanied by three men. I guess they were Masters as well. Mistress Robyn and one of the Masters stood behind Elyse, Mistress Kimberly and one of the Masters stood behind Justine and Mistress Yvonne and one of the Masters stood behind me. I don't recall when they came in or maybe they came in when the lights were out, but three female slaves rubbed oils all over our bodies. It smelled like lavender. They placed blindfolds on us.

I could hear them talking in the background, but couldn't make out what they were saying. Then I heard the sounds of the whips cracking lightly behind us. It was sort of nerve wrecking. A whip has never struck me ever in my life. I was so afraid I was shaking. However I was also excited. My entire body was on edge. I was almost in a panic trying to anticipate the first strike.

I don't remember hearing them stop cracking the whips. All I know is I felt something strike my shoulder and I let out a scream that scared even me. What actually happened was my Mistress came up behind me and placed her hand on my shoulder. I startled her as well, causing her to let out a scream.

Mistress tied my hair up so it was off my back. She leaned in and whispered in my ear, "Are you alright?" She tried not to laugh, but she couldn't help herself.

I didn't think it was all that funny. I answered with a shaky voice, "Yes Mistress I'm alright."

Mistress finally stopped laughing. "I know this was sprung on you. If you're not up to this let me know."

"I trust you. I'll be alright." I really do trust Mistress, but I wasn't quite sure how I would hold up.

Mistress checked the ropes around my waist and the hook. "I'm going to give you three safe words. You can use them at any time you need for me to stop or slow down. *'Green'* means everything is all right and you want me to keep going. So if I ask if you are all right, you can just say *'Green'* and I will know you are all right. *'Yellow'* means you are all right, but you need for me to slow down. *'Red'* means you need for me to stop. You can use these safe words at any time. Do you understand?"

"Yes Mistress. Green means I'm all right and keep going. Yellow means I want you to slow down and red means I need for you to stop."

"Very good," Mistress kissed my neck. "I know we haven't used safe words before so if you forget them and need for me to stop, just tell me to stop."

"Yes Mistress. But I will not forget."

Mistress stepped away. Next Mistress Kimberly stepped up and had a similar conversation with Justine. Afterwards Mistress Robyn had a similar conversation with Elyse.

A few minutes later the whips started cracking again in the background. Only this time they were getting closer. I could feel the air rush against my skin from the force of the crack of the whip. It felt as if my heart got stuck in my throat.

For a brief moment the whips fell silent. Then in perfect sync all three whips cracked and found their targets. The tip of Mistress Yvonne's whip snapped on my left butt cheek. All three of us squealed in harmony. A second crack of her whip's tip snapped across my right cheek with equal force.

The three of us squirmed trying our best to escape the next anticipated lash. The ropes held us firmly to one another. Our legs were free, but the more we kicked the more the hooks which were buried deep within our pussies tugged against us. We tried in vain to remain motionless. The more any of us moved our hips to the side, the more the hooks dug in and tugged against us.

The first time the tip snapped against the middle of my back it sent shock waves throughout my entire body. The strokes weren't hard. They were at a steady pace, with brief pauses to allow the sensation to radiate throughout our bodies.

After about five minutes the female slaves removed our blindfolds. The one attending me turned my head so she can look into my eyes. She then asked, "How are you holding up?"

"I answered. "I'm fine."

She then asked, "Do you wish to continue?"

"Green," I answered.

She nodded to my Mistress and then stepped away without replacing my blindfold. The female slaves attending Justine and Elyse did the same. Justine and I were scared out of our wits. However, Elyse's eyes had excitement in them. Don't get me wrong. I was excited as well, as I'm sure Justine was. But it was different for Elyse. Each stroke seemed to enhance her excitement.

She even started to taunt her Mistress, "Harder, faster."

As Mistress Robyn intensified her efforts, Elyse's reactions became even more animated. Every movement she made tugged and pulled us along with her as the whips from our own Mistresses beckoned us in opposing directions. Soon the hook was acting as a Vibrator, pulsating hard against the back of my clitoris. My orgasm triggered Justine's orgasm.

Elyse was however in another place. I could tell from her eyes she was experiencing something totally different than Justine and I. I noticed the slave assigned to her paying close attention to her. After Mistress Yvonne and Mistress Kimberly set their whips down, Mistress Robyn continued. Soon all three slaves were attending Elyse. One even gave Elyse ice to suck on.

After about ten minutes one of the slaves motioned to Mistress Robyn to stop. She complied immediately. Elyse looked as if she was totally out of it. They watched Elyse for several minutes, then lowered us to the ground and untied us.

My Mistress came over and walked me over to a sofa in the corner. She held me in her arms. My entire body was so sensitized her very touch excited me. I never felt this way in my entire life. Last night came close but this was different. Mistress has punished me a lot more severely than this in the past.

But this wasn't a punishment. I never imagined a bullwhip could be so sensual and erotic at the same time. Physically I was spent. But at the same time I had this burst of sexual energy. I had never been so horny in my entire life. All I wanted to do was devour my Mistress.

I straddled her and gave her the most passionate kiss I could muster. Looking back I surprised even myself at how aggressive I became. I pinned her down and gave her the longest kiss I could before we both had to come up gasping for air.

I let down my hair and attempted to strip that latex outfit off my Mistress. I let out this primal screech in frustration. This fucking suit was unyielding and deprived me from the pleasures of my Mistress.

My head must have been someplace else. My Mistress sat up, reached back and unzipped her suit. How in the hell did I miss a zipper down the middle of her back? I was about to attack her again when she turned over, straddled me and pushed me onto my back. She put her finger to my lips and whispered, "Ralentizar mi amor."

She stood up and slowly removed her gloves. She tossed them at me one by one as she peeled them off. I never felt so excited in my entire life. My entire body was throbbing with sexual tension and excitement.

She placed her right foot on top of the sofa directly over my head. She leaned in and slowly unzipped her boot as her top fell slightly off her left shoulder. She stepped out of her boot and let it fall to the sofa next to me.

She then lowered her right leg and placed her left foot on the sofa, right up against my crotch. She pushed the tip of her shoe right up against me until it ever so slightly penetrated me. She leaned forward and allowed her top to fall completely off both her shoulders, exposing her sweaty breasts to me. She slowly unzipped her boot and stepped out of it, allowing it to fall to the ground.

She stepped back and slowly peeled the latex body suit off and stepped free of it. I was so worked up all I could do was cry at the sight of her perfect body. She leaned in towards me slowly. Before she could get the upper hand I took control. I pulled her in towards me forcing her off balance. I forced her on her back and straddled her face. Her tongue was electric. It sent shockwaves throughout my body, I never cum so quickly in my life.

I wasn't done with her by a long shot. I worked my way down her body caressing every inch of her with my kisses. Her nipples were erect and especially sensitive so I paid extra attention to them. When I finally made my way to her inner most thighs I could tell she had cum several times already. I was sure to clean up every drop before turning my full attention to her clit. I love it when I drive Mistress mad with ecstasy.

Afterwards I lay in her arms as I played with the leash attached to my collar. I noticed for the first time that even though I was butt naked, as long as I wore Mistress' collar I didn't feel naked, it makes me feel safe, she makes me feel safe. I wonder what makes her feel safe. I wonder if she feels the same for me as I feel for her.

I lay in my Mistress' arms for about an hour. She stroked my hair and looked down at me. "You know I love you, right?"

I looked up at her, "Yes Mistress. I know you love me, as I love you."

"Things are going to change. I've been way too soft on you. You say you want to serve me 24/7. Are you sure that is what you want?"

I fell a little faint and speechless. My only desire is to serve my Mistress totally. But hearing it from her lips made it real. My voice cracked slightly as I answered, "Yes Mistress. I wish to serve you totally."

My Mistress looked down at me. "I'm talking about a Total Power Exchange."

"Are Justine and Elyse still my sister slaves?"

"Yes," Mistress answered.

"What is my position with them? I mean just how does that work?" I was hoping Mistress would say that I was he slave and since she was number one, I was number one amongst my sister slaves as well. Of course she didn't say that.

"When the three of you are together and not serving your Mistress you will be expected to watch out for each other. You will have to work out your positions amongst yourselves, Babe Gurl."

"When do we begin Mistress?"

"Now." Mistress removed the leash from my collar. Suddenly two huge masked men dressed in all black yanked me to my feet by my arms.

In Her Service

My imagination raced wildly as the two men dragged me down the hallway. I was in such distress I failed to notice Justine and Elyse were also being escorted down the hallway with me. We were taken to the medical office where Matt was awaiting us. We were laid face down on three separate medical beds.

Three female nurses cleaned our backs and then placed ointment on our marks. It stung a little, but not a lot. Matt didn't speak to us as he inspected the nurses' work.

After he was satisfied with their work, he dismissed them and broke his silence. "I will return with and inspect you in about an hour." He left before we could respond.

"What the fuck happens next?" I asked. I was sort of excited, but I guess it came out wrong.

Elyse snapped at me, "What did I tell you about your mouth? Don't worry about what happens next. Just learn to do as you are told."

I think I was hurt more by Justine's response. "Don't fuck this up. I don't believe what happened between Uwa and you. What the fuck was you thinking?" Her tone was very self-righteous.

I snapped back, "I made a mistake with Uwa. Besides I know you would fuck Uwa if you had the chance."

"I don't give a fuck about Uwa you stupid cunt." I never heard Justine this upset before. "You are not true to yourself. How can you serve Mistress Yvonne, until you know what you want? If you want to fuck Uwa, fuck Uwa. Just stop the games."

"I want Mistress, not Uwa or anyone else for that matter." I replied.

Elyse asked, "We know you want her. But do you want her as your Mistress or merely s a lover?"

"Why can't I have both?" I asked.

"You can't serve a lover. But you can love your Mistress." Elyse answered.

Justine got up and walked over and knelt down at my head. "She's in love with you. That's dangerous for a Mistress to be in love with her slave."

"Why is that?" I asked.

"She holds back. She doubts herself." Justine stated.

"She's afraid you are too fragile and can't take it." Elyse added.

"You have to show her you are stronger than you act. I know you are a fucking pain slut, just as I am." Justine added and then kissed my forehead.

"How do I do that?" I asked.

"You serve your Mistress in all things as if no one other Mistress or Master exists," Elyse responded.

Justine looked into my eyes. "As your sister slaves we shall watch your back and kick your ass if you fall short."

"What if I fail?" I really wasn't asking a question. I was just thinking out loud.

"You can't fail. It's not a test." Justine answered. "Just be yourself."

I really didn't know what to do with that. I don't really know who I am or what I want. I know I love Mistress Yvonne and I want to serve her. I just not entirely sure what that mean?

We spent the rest of the time mostly in silence until Matt returned. He inspected us and gave us gowns to wear back to our dorm. We were all drained and we slept past diner.

I didn't see Mistress until the next morning at breakfast. I was sore all over and I could still feel those hooks inside of me. After breakfast Mistress kept me chained to my post until everyone else left the dinning area.

Once everyone else, except for the staff, left Mistress ordered, "Strip." And then she walked off and out of the room.

Every male staff member seemed to stare intently at me as I undressed. I have walked around the dungeon many times completely naked. I don't know why I was so self-conscious.

Mistress returned about ten minutes later. She didn't say anything. She unchained me and connected a leather leash to my collar. She led me down the hallway to the lower dungeon. Everyone was already there.

Mistress led me to the front where there was a table with the dreaded bitch suit. "On your back slut and get those knees up." Mistress ordered as she removed my collar.

I took my ordered position. Mistress dressed me in the bitch suit. This suit was a little different. It was a tight fitting black latex suit. It had a hood but it also had a snout with a built in o-ring. Mistress turned me over so I was on my elbows and knees. She put my collar and leash back around my neck.

I prepared myself for the insertion of the butt plug tail. My Mistress just walked away and left me exposed and on display. Uwa followed her. I couldn't see where they went. When they returned Uwa was carrying a metal bucket filled with soapy water. He set it down directly in front of me. I could see the steam rising from it. Mistress was holding what looked like a giant syringe with a tapered metal tip.

"When you have a bitch who needs taming you sometimes have to get creative in your punishments." Mistress held up the object in her hand. "You can carry out this form of punishment with a traditional enema kit, but this device allows you to force the solution deeper into her bowels at a much faster rate. It is just as uncomfortable going as it is holding the solution inside."

Uwa stirred the water until it was very sudsy.

Mistress continued. "I'm using a warm water, with a mild liquid soap. You have to make sure the water isn't too hot. You don't want to burn the little bitch. But you want it warm enough that she understands this is a punishment."

I watched as Mistress slowly filled the device with the soapy water. She shoved the un-lubricated nozzle deep inside my ass. I bolted as the soapy water gushed deep inside of me, warming my insides as it worked its way through my bowels. Uwa held me securely in place.

Mistress wasted little time in refilling her device and forcing even more of the solution deeper into my aching bowels. I felt as if I was going to burst wide open. Mistress forced another dose inside of me and quickly sealed my ass with a large butt plug tail. She then led me around the dungeon several times by my leash. Every movement was pure agony. I could hear the solution sloshing around inside of me. Each time I slowed down Mistress gave me ten solid swats with her riding crop. I tried my best to keep up, but I must have earned at least fifty swats.

Mistress finally led me back to the front of the class. She made me lean forward with my arms stretched out as far in front of me as I can get them while resting on my elbows. My legs were spread shoulder width apart forcing my ass up in the air and completely exposed. I could feel the solution pressing working its way through me.

I started whimpering in total agony. Justine and Elyse started glaring at me and slightly shaking their heads no. So I did my best to remain quiet. I tried to focus on Justine's face. It worked for a while, until I felt Mistress fingering me.

The most embarrassing part wasn't being exposed like that, it was when a gurgling sound started coming from my stomach. I could feel the solution starting to work its way back up and pushing against the unyielding butt plug tail.

Mistress pulled my head up by placing her hand under my chin as she spoke, "As you can see this position has my little slut bitch completely immobile and completely at my mercy. As you can see

131

by the expression in her eyes, this is extremely uncomfortable for her."

I saw Elyse mouth the word focus to me. I did my best to focus on her and Justine.

Then Mistress put this thing in front of my face. "This is a wand." Mistress stated. She flicked a switch and it started making a low hum and then blue electrical arches started forming between the two prongs on the tip of the wand.

At this point I was on the edge of total panic. I forgot my fucking colors. I looked over at Justine for help. Justine looked up at Mistress Kimberly and then up at Mistress Yvonne. She then crawled over to me. Mistress released her grip on me and Justine lifted my head up in her hands.

Justine told me, "Slow down your breathing so you don't hyperventilate."

I did my best to control my breathing.

Justine continued. "Good girl. Do you remember your safe words?"

I shook my head no.

Justine wiped the tears from my eyes. "Red means stop. Yellow means slow down and green means you are all right and your Mistress may continue. Do you want to stop?"

I shook my head no. Some how, now that I knew my safe words I was able to calm down.

"Do you need a break?"

I shook my head no.

Justine kissed me on my forehead. "I'll be right here." She gently placed my head back down on the ground.

Mistress continued her lecture. "I want the Dominates to come around to the back so you can see what I'm doing."

The Dominates got up and walked around behind me.

Mistress continued. "The wand will not hurt or electrocute your slave. As you can see you don't have to make direct contact for the wand to be effective."

I thought I was prepared for what was about to happen. But, Mistress caught me totally off guard. She moved the wand over that place between my pussy and ass hole. The shockwave raced through my entire body. I let out a yelp. I definitely felt the shock, but it didn't hurt.

Mistress continued, "Did you see how the electricity arched from the wand to her ass?"

I could hear several voices behind me answering yes. The demonstration didn't last long. She only used the wand on me about three additional times over the next five minutes. I know it sounds strange but I was relieved when the shocks came. It was pure torture waiting for the next one.

At the end of the session Mistress led me by my leash down the hallway to the toilet. Before we entered the toilet she removed the bitch suit but not the butt plug tail. My jaw was sore from the o-ring that was made into the snout.

Mistress stood me up, replaced my collar and removed the leash. "When you are finished relieving yourself, be sure to clean your tail. Take it back to our room and put it with your other toys. Don't bother getting dressed. Then go back to your room and wait I will send for you."

"Yes Mistress." I replied.

Mistress walked away. I wanted to run into the toilet, but every step was a challenge. I'm not going to go into details about my ordeal in relieving myself. Although no one saw me, I know anyone passing by could hear. It was extremely embarrassing. I washed the butt plug tail as instructed. As I was ready to leave I could feel another wave of water rushing its way out of my bowels. I raced back to the toilet just in time.

The walk back to the main mansion was longer than usual. I could still feel some of the soapy water sloshing around inside of me. Of course Maria was there when finally arrived. I raced past her and headed for the nearest toilet to relieve myself. When I came out she just rolled her eyes at me and smiled to herself. I wish I knew what I had done to her.

I was totally drained. I needed to refresh myself. I took a quick shower, put on a pair of flip-flops and went back to my dorm. Taking a shower before I headed back may have been a mistake. My skin was damp and there was a cool breeze.

When I got back to the dorm I kicked off the flip-flops and crawled into bed. I didn't bother getting under the covers. The room was warm and getting under the covers would have taken too much energy.

New Beginnings

I don't know how long I was asleep. I was awoken by a sharp slap across my ass. Of course Justine was standing over me.

"Are you going to sleep your life away?" she said with a smile on her face.

"Oh fuck, how long was I asleep?" I jumped up. "I have to get dinner."

"Don't worry about it. Your Mistress wanted you to sleep in."

"Why didn't someone come and get me?"

"You were out to the world. How do you feel?"

"I don't know. That was fucking intense."

Justine picked up a dress from her bed and tossed it to me. "Slip this on. Your shoes are next to your bed. We have to be out front in three minutes." Justine started undressing. "We are going out for dinner."

The dress was beautiful. It was a lavender silk pleated Dior Chiffon dress. It wasn't a full-length gown. It only came a little above mid-thigh. When I sat down to put on my shoes the dress rose up over my ass. The shoes were a pair of black Dior stud caged sandals with four-inch heels and one-inch platforms.

Justine also wore a silk Dior Chiffon dress. It was a different design, but about the same length. She also wore Dior shoes. Just as we finished dressing Elyse opened the door, "Lets go." She was also in a Dior silk Chiffon dress.

"Where are we going?" I asked.

"Still asking questions Babe Gurl?" Elyse asked.

I didn't answer. I just walked out the door. Justine followed. When we got out front Mistress Yvonne, Kimberly and Robyn were standing next to the limo waiting. They were in full-length silk

135

Dior chiffon gowns. I don't know if they were real or not, but they were wearing gorgeous necklace, earrings and bracelets.

"Front and center ladies and lift up those dresses." Mistress Robyn ordered.

We walked over and stood in front of our Mistress and raised the hems of our dresses above our hips. None of us were wearing any panties. Our Mistresses opened one of two boxes they were holding and pulled out two steel balls. They inserted them inside our pussies. They were cold. They sort of vibrated a little when they hit each other.

After they pulled our dresses down and adjusted them, they opened the second larger box. I couldn't believe it. It was a diamond choker with matching earrings. I don't know if they were real or not, I really didn't care they looked great. They removed collars and placed the necklaces around our necks and the earrings on our ears.

Of course Justine had to ask. "Are these real?"

"Of course they are real." Mistress Kimberly answered. "Everything here is real, get use to it."

I never had diamonds before. This was awesome. I had to fight to holdback the tears. I managed to keep my composure. I asked, "Where are we going Mistress?"

"It's a surprise." Mistress responded. She kissed me softly on my lips. "Now get in. We don't want to be late."

We got into the limo. It was nice and warm. Our Mistresses sat next to us. There was a table in front of us. There was an opened bottle of Champaign in an ice bucket. There were also six filled Champaign glasses surrounded by large chocolate dipped strawberries and loose long stem roses. Our Mistresses picked up two glasses and gave one to each of us.

Mistress Yvonne raised her glass. "To us ladies. This is our night."

We all raised our glasses and said cheers. I don't know what we were celebrating, but I was excited. It was a smooth drive. I barely felt when the driver pulled off. I don't remember what we talked about. But we didn't speak as Mistress and slave. We spoke as if we were a close group of friends out for a night on the town.

It was a very intimate and romantic ride. There was a smoked glass divider separating us from the driver. The windows in the back were blacked out so no one could look in, but we could look out. The lighting was soft and there was soft music playing in the background. Mistress kept her hand on my thigh most of the ride. I was hoping she would go a little higher. But she didn't.

When we arrived, it was more than I could have ever imagined. When our limo stopped, men dressed in black tuxedos opened our door. Mistress Kimberly opened a cabinet and handed each of us a wrap that matched the dresses we were wearing. She also handed out wraps to Mistress Yvonne and Mistress Robyn. The men who opened the door to our limo held out their hand and guided each of us out of the limo. Mistress Yvonne and I walked into the hotel, followed by Mistress Kimberly and Justine, who were followed by Mistress Robyn and Elyse.

Those balls they placed inside of us started bumping into each other as I walked. They worked their way deeper inside of me with each step. They started bumping against the top walls of my pussy against the underside of my clitoris. It made it hard to keep up at times.

When we entered the reception area we were escorted to a Ballroom complete with crystal chandeliers. We were seated at the head table. A few minutes later Master Adams and Mistress Julie entered. Mistress Kelly and Uwa along with Mistress Cleo and Mistress Sheila and their male slaves entered and were escorted to the head table as well. We were seated in our normal positions. The only difference was that there were no perches. We sat to the left of our Mistresses.

I looked out as Masters and Mistresses along with their slaves and submissive entered and were escorted to their seats. A few of them

I recognized from the dungeon. Most of them I had never seen before.

After everyone was seated and the doors were closed Mistress Julie stood up and clinked her crystal wine glass with a fork. The room became silent almost instantly.

Mistress Julie put her glass and the fork down. "I want to welcome each of you as we celebrate the christening of our newest mansion, Palais Maîtresse de Douleur et de Plaisir. The mansion will be managed by Mistress Kelly and Mistress Yvonne."

Everyone applauded.

Mistress Julie continued. "They will be assisted by Mistress Cleo, Mistress Sheila, Mistress Kelly and Mistress Robyn."

Applause echoed throughout the ballroom again.

Mistress Julie waited until the applause died down. She raised her glass that was now filled with Champaign. We raised our glasses as well. "Hommage à la Maîtresse Palais de Douleur et de Plaisir."

I have no idea what she said. I didn't do too well in French. Dinner was excellent. For the first time in a long time I actually fed myself with a knife and fork.

After dinner we danced. I was doing just fine until someone requested the band play a Salsa. Mistress goes all out when she dances a Salsa. It's all I can do to keep up with her under normal circumstances. But those fucking balls kept banging together and viberating until I collapsed in Mistress' arms in the mist of a full on orgasm. Although no one seemed to notice, I know they knew.

Mistress held me in her arms in the middle of the dance floor until I was able to regain my composure. It felt nice to be held by her and to hold her in my arms. She was wearing my favorite perfume.

Mistress whispered in my ear. "I'm very proud of you. You held up very well."

I looked up at her. "I'm sorry about Uwa. I don't know what came over me. I promise to stay clear of him."

"That will be hard to do, since you will be working with him."

"I promise to never let you down again Mistress."

Mistress stroked my hair. "Face it. You are a slut Sara McNeil. But you are my slut. And if you ever forget that again, you will pay with your ass. Is that clear?"

"Yes Mistress." I replied softly.

I laid my head on her shoulder and we danced for what seemed like hours. I don't know what Mistress sees in me. I have failed her in almost everyway. I have never seen her so happy. This means so much to her and Mistress is everything to me. I don't know what live at the mansion will be like, but I will serve my Mistress to the best of my ability.